This Wonderful Universe

This edition published 2025
by Living Book Press
Copyright © Living Book Press, 2025

ISBN: 978-1-76153-851-3 (hardcover)
        978-1-76153-810-0 (softcover)

First published in 1897.

A catalogue record for this book is available from the National Library of Australia

This Wonderful Universe

by

AGNES GIBERNE

COULD THE SUN approach to where the MOON IS, then at any
instant great crimson "FLAMES" of hydrogen gas might leap forth
and enwrap our little EARTH in their fervid embrace.

Contents

FOREWORD TO NEW EDITION

MANY years ago, a small volume under this title was published by the S.P.C.K. When a letter came, asking me to revise it for re-issue in an illustrated form, I speedily found that to "revise" meant to "re-write." And re-written it has been during the past few months, with abundant omissions and still more abundant additions. Except possibly here or there in the first few pages, I doubt if a single sentence has kept its old form unaltered. And though, in the main, I have roughly followed the outlines of my former plan, it has been largely reconstructed, and very many of the chapters are entirely new.

I have to express my grateful thanks to Mr. W. H. Wesley, Assistant Secretary of the Royal Astronomical society; Mr. E. Walter Maunder, F.R.A.S.; Professor H. H. Turner, F.R.S., Director of the University Observatory of Oxford; Professor E. B. Frost, Director of Yerkes Observatory, Wisconsin; Mr. Harlow Shapley, of Mount Wilson Observatory, California; and others, for most kind help given in the work of re-writing, by their ready response to inquiries on my part about difficult questions and new developments.

My thanks also are due to several poets of the present day, whose names will be found here and there, as well as to their publishers, for leave kindly granted for the use of their poems both in this and in a companion volume on the subject of Plant-life, which is to appear a little later. So, while the latter will be about flowers on our Earth, this one is about more flaming blossoms in the Garden of the Skies. As wrote Erasmus Wilson, long ago -

> "Flowers of the sky; ye too to age must yield,
> Frail as your silken sisters of the field."

In both books, I have given quotations not only from modern poets but from many of bygone generations. It is always interesting to note the manner in which great scientific truths are received by widely differing minds, gifted with poetic insight. Perhaps not least so with writers of a past age, when that which was known, alike of life on our small world and of conditions in the great Universe, could hardly be compared with what is known to us now.

AGNES GIBERNE.

PART I

OUR OUTLOOK FROM EARTH

I. - A RAPID WHIRL

ONCE upon a time, a man is reported to have said: "Don't tell *me* that the world goes round. I know better. 'Cause why? When I get up in the morning, I see the very same view all round as when I went to bed."

That man, at all events, thought for himself, which is better than not thinking at all, even though his thinking led to a mistaken conclusion. And the reasoning was not out of place. Nay, he had hold of an important truth; only he used that truth wrongly.

He grasped the fact that a man, going from one spot to another, must from time to time have different things about him. If he walks, the changes come slowly; if he travels by train, they arrive more quickly. In any case, he cannot pass onward, hour after hour, moving among objects which do not move, and still see the same houses, the same trees, the same fields, the same hills. As he advances, he leaves the old surroundings behind and finds himself amid new surroundings.

The man, of course, knew this. Though not learned in scientific matters, he had his share of common sense. When somebody told him that our solid old world was not, as he supposed, quietly at rest, but was incessantly twirling like a teetotum, he began to use his common sense.

He knew that when he went to bed at night, he could see certain objects in the country around; and he knew that when he woke up in the morning, he would find those same objects, each in exactly the same position. Then he put two and two together and decided that the notion of the Earth spinning must be a mistake.

"Don't tell *me*," he said. "I know better!"

And all the time, he was himself making a curious mistake. Up to a certain point, his reasoning was not incorrect; but he looked in the wrong direction for the changes of scene which he rightly considered ought to come about. And rather oddly, while taking it for granted that *he* would move with the moving Earth, he does not seem to have faced the probability that other objects on Earth's surface would do the same.

It never occurred to him that not only his own little house and garden and everything in them, but other houses with all that they contained, and trees and fields, hedges and ponds, hills and valleys — one and all must be carried onward just as fast as the surface of the Earth was moving. Otherwise, if everything were left behind by that rushing surface, it would mean a complete and terrific jumble of destruction.

Naturally, therefore, the view before his eyes each morning had to be the same as his view of the evening before.

When a man in a railway carriage is borne along at the rate of fifty miles an hour, all that is inside that carriage travels at the same pace. The cushions, the seats, the people, the luggage, the fly on a windowpane, the air which fills the compartment — all are journeying at fifty miles an hour. And when a traveller wishes to find a changing scene, he must not fix his gaze on the floor, or the seats, or on a fellow traveller. He must look *outside* at the fields, the trees, the houses, the villages seen through the windows.

This is just what one on Earth must do if he would discover the movements of our globe from changes in the scenery. He must look right outside, away from Earth altogether; not at the things on our world, which move with the Earth as he does himself. And that is exactly what the man did not do. He looked only at the things around, all journeying with himself, and he forgot to gaze away *outside*, away from the hurrying surface of the solid globe on which he stood.

"Ah, yes," perhaps you may say. "He ought to have looked right off from everything on the ground. He ought to have watched the clouds. Then he would have understood."

No; not even then. That would have meant a second mistake on his part.

It is true that he would not usually find precisely the same clouds as the evening before, because clouds are perpetually altering their shapes, melting away, reforming, taking new outlines. But these changes in them would be real. They would not be *seeming* changes brought about by his own movements.

The clouds would have travelled onward, as he did himself, with the Earth's surface. They might be blown hither and thither by currents of air; but *as a* whole, they would have been carried from west to east by the steady whirl of the entire atmosphere, which moves with the surface of the Earth.

So if the man wished to get a really outside view, he would have to look beyond the clouds, beyond the great deep ocean of air, which really is a part of our Earth. He would have to lift his gaze into the sky, where float the Moon and Sun, the planets, and the stars. Then, at last, he would find scenery which seems to change, like the objects noticed out of a rushing train — objects which often cannot but seem to move, if this world really does move, because they are not a part of the Earth, as air and clouds, hills and towns, fields, rivers, and oceans are.

> "Now glowed the firmament
> With living sapphires; Hesperus, that led
> The starry host, rode brightest, till the Moon,
> Rising in clouded majesty, at length
> Apparent queen unveiled her peerless light,
> And o'er the dark her silver mantle threw."
>
> MILTON: *Paradise Lost.*

II. - HEAVENLY BODIES.

The first and simplest idea which a child generally has of Earth and sky is of a wide, flat plain, and of a fixed sky above, with clouds and a sun in it by day, and a moon and stars in it by night. Stars always at night, when the sky is clear; and a sun always by day, unless hidden by clouds; but a moon not always after dark.

So much as this, an intelligent child might be expected to find out for himself, even if not told. And the first men who inhabited this Earth must have seen such things very much as an untaught child now would see them. Probably this was the idea in the mind of the man who could not believe that the Earth revolved.

But suppose that, instead of making up his mind in such a hurry, he had taken time to watch and to think. Suppose he had glanced away from Earth to the heavens, far beyond cloudland; had looked, not once or twice only, and not carelessly, but day after day with attentive and earnest eyes. Suppose he had kept this up week after week, month after month, even year after year, trying to find out what changes in that heavenly scenery might mean.

He would see what already he knew — that the Sun, each morning, comes up from below the easterly horizon, crosses the sky — higher up or lower down at different seasons — and goes down below the westerly horizon. He would notice that the Moon, by night, when visible, does much the same; rising somewhere in the east, crossing part of the sky, and setting somewhere in the west.

He would find the stars also to be on the move, many of them, like the Sun and Moon, rising in an easterly direction, crossing the sky, and setting in a westerly direction. A certain number, toward the north, are never seen from our part of the Earth to set but keep circling round and round a certain point.

Then, if left to himself, with no books or teachers and no help from the thousands of years during which other men before him have watched, waited, studied, and found explanations, he would doubtless fall into the same mistakes that men of ancient days fell into long ago.

He would feel sure that this flat Earth, on which he had a footing, which feels so firm and solid, must certainly be at rest. Therefore, he would feel no less sure that the whole sky, with Sun, Moon, and hosts of stars, must be whirling round and round our Earth, once in every twenty-four hours.

That would indeed be a tremendous feat for the heavens to perform! Wonderful things are done in the sky, but nothing quite so utterly and hopelessly beyond all human imagination as this!

Only, in far-back days, it was not beyond imagination, because men then knew so very little of the real size of our marvellous universe or of the enormous numbers of stars contained in it, or of the stupendous distances which divide its stars one from another. To the mind of a man in those times, it was much more difficult to imagine that our world could spin day and night like a huge top than that the entire heavens should perpetually whirl round and round us.

Of the two explanations, one had to be true; and it was just a question of which was the easier to accept. Men believed that which seemed to them the simpler.

Now that we know better what would be meant by such a whirl, we realise how much simpler and easier the explanation is, founded on the idea of our small Earth's daily turning on her own axis.

Astronomers gradually discovered that many other bodies in the sky — the Sun, for instance, and the planets — are steadily spinning or revolving, each on its own axis, some more quickly, some more slowly. Examined through a telescope, they are clearly seen to do so. And if other bodies, many of them far larger than this world, are known to behave thus, why not the Earth also? The idea, far from looking impossible, has become an everyday fact.

When once we grant that our world is ever spinning round and round, carrying with her everything on and near her surface, then the daily movements of the Sun, the nightly movements of the Moon and stars, are explained. We see them *seem* to move merely because we ourselves are moving. We see them *seem* to come up from the east and go down in the west because we on Earth are being carried from west to east. It is much the same as when a man, journeying in a train from north to south, sees trees, fields, and villages appear to travel from south to north.

Not that this particular movement, this daily whirl of our Earth, is her only movement! And not that the Sun, Moon, planets, and stars have no real movements of their own! But just now, all we have to do with is the fact that the daily and nightly whirl of the skies around us is not real. It is only an appearance, brought about by the ceaseless spin of our small Earth. Other movements may be left alone for a while.

> "Mysterious Night; when our first parent knew
>   Thee from report Divine, and heard thy name,
>   Did he not tremble for this lovely frame,
> This glorious canopy of light and dew?
>
> "Yet 'neath a curtain of translucent dew,
>   Bathed in the rays of the great setting flame,
>   Hesperus with the host of heaven came,
> And lo, Creation widened in man's view.
>
> "Who could have thought such darkness lay concealed
> Within thy beams, O Sun? Or who could find,
>   Whilst fly and leaf and insect stood revealed,
> That to such countless orbs thou mad'st us blind?
>   Why do we then shun Death with anxious strife?
>   If Light can thus deceive, wherefore not Life?"
>
> BLANCO WHITE

III. – THE SHAPE OF OUR EARTH

A man standing on the equator is carried, in the course of twenty-four hours, right round under the entire heavens. If he were gazing through all those hours steadily up into the sky, he might view the whole landscape of stars visible from this world — but for one hindrance. That hindrance is the radiance of sunlight, which in daytime shuts off the dim flicker of starlight. Could he cover up the Sun, and so secure twenty-four hours of darkness, he might survey all at a single stretch.

Not that the heavens would journey round him while he stood on a fixed and motionless world, but that he, on the whirling surface of our revolving globe, would be carried round swiftly under each part of the sky in turn, travelling always from west to east.

But a man standing farther north or farther south, and not on the equator, would not gain so full a view. Portions of the heavens would be hidden from him by the intervening solid body of the Earth.

There are many stars over the region of the south pole, which we in Britain and in other northern parts of Europe and North America can never see. And there are many stars over the region of the north pole, which people in southern Australia and south Africa can never see. It is only from the equator that a man might obtain a complete view.

Since the Earth is not, as was once supposed, a flat plain reaching to endless distances, but a round globe or sphere, its surface curves away from us, wherever we happen to be, till it passes out of sight at the horizon line. The curve is very gentle, but it is found in all parts of the world alike.

A very interesting proof of the round shape of our Earth is given in an eclipse of the Moon.

Sometimes, in our yearly journeying around the Sun — this is another of the Earth's movements — we pass exactly between the Sun and the Moon so that the three bodies are in a direct line. More often, it happens that either the Sun or the Moon is just a little higher or a little lower, and then the three are not in a line. But when it does so come about, the Sun casts a shadow of the Earth upon the Moon. And since the latter shines only by reflected sunlight, she at once becomes dim.

And — note this! — the shadow thrown by our Earth is a *round* shadow. As the grey shade creeps slowly over the bright Moon-face, it is always a *rounded edge* which moves onward. No matter which part of the Earth casts its shadow, the result is the same. England, India, Australia, America — these or other countries may face the Moon; but invariably the creeping shadow is round in shape, and the back edge following is round also.

If you hold up an orange between a lighted lamp and the wall — rather near the wall, and not too near the lamp — you will see that the shadow thrown by it is a round shadow. Turn it about as you will, offer one side after another to the lamp, and still the shadow will be round.

Then hold up a flat plate to the lamp, and you will find that the shape of the shadow depends on how you place it. In one position, and one only, it will cast a round shadow. In others, the shadow will be more or less oval; while, if you hold the plate *edgeways* towards the lamp, the shadow becomes only a straight, broadish line.

Do you see how strong a proof is given here as to the shape of the Earth? And it is one that comes again and again, every time we have an eclipse of the Moon.

And now about the size of the little world on which we live.

If a road could be made straight through its center, from one side to the other, perhaps on the equator, such a road would be nearly eight thousand miles long. A carriage drawn by quick horses, going at the rate of ten miles an hour, never lessening speed by day or night, might accomplish that distance in thirty-three days, or just over a calendar month. A train or a motor car, traveling fifty miles an hour, without a single break, might do the same in less than a week.

But with horses and engines, not to speak of passengers, halts are needed. And when we romance about going down into the Earth and out on the further side, in any such fashion, we are talking about an unknown region. The outside surface of our globe is more or less familiar; but not the inside.

A recent statement gives as the greatest depth of a mine ever yet sunk "the No. 3 shaft of the Tamarack mine in the county Michigan," which "reached a vertical depth of about 5,200 feet," that is, slightly under one mile. A mere scratching of Earth's crust! Even if we suggest a larger margin and say that no mine has reached a depth beyond two miles — what are two miles compared with eight thousand? True, parts of our ocean bottoms lie six or even seven miles below the ocean surface; but those depths are far beyond our reach.

Imagine what it would mean to delve four thousand miles below the surface of our Earth; four thousand miles away from light and air; nearly four thousand miles beneath our oceans. And to complicate matters, the inside of our world is believed to be intensely heated; so much so, according to one authority, that about thirty miles down the heat must be great enough to melt all solid rocks. If they are not there in an actually molten state, it is only because the immense pressure tends to keep them solid.

Such a road would indeed utterly dwarf the grandest engineering works of man.

Though a road of this kind is impossible, and though we cannot hope ever to dig or blast our way downwards until the opposite side is reached, yet the actual size of our Earth has been again and again reckoned. The size of any globe, both through the middle and around the outside, may always be found out from careful measurements of parts of its surface. The work of surveyors comes in here, and such measurements have been made countless times, with calculations worked out from them.

We now know, as a matter of certainty, that the Earth is about eight thousand miles through from pole to pole or from side to side straight through the center, and about twenty-five thousand miles around at the equator.

By the "equator" we mean an imaginary line around the Earth, halfway between the north and south poles. And when we speak of the north pole or the south pole *in the heavens*, we mean always that point in the sky which lies just over our Earth's north pole or our Earth's south pole.

With regard to the shape of our Earth, it is, as already stated, a globe or ball. More strictly, it is like an orange, since it has slightly flattened poles. In scientific language, the Earth is an "oblate spheroid;" and in connection with this term, a little scene of past days comes to mind.

My father one day was showing cube shapes to two little girls, aged about nine and seven, explaining their names and uses. In a corner of the room, their small sister, only three and a half or possibly as much as four years old, was seated on the floor, playing happily with her toys.

Presently, to see how far his explanations had been understood, my father asked a question or two, and among them, "What is the shape of our Earth?"

Seven-years-old and nine-years-old tried to remember. But the baby in the corner, busied with her dolls, had listened to some purpose, and the pause was broken by a sweet little treble voice piping out — "An *oblate spheroid*, uncle!"

My father's surprise and amusement may well be imagined.

And perhaps I cannot do better than mention here how deep is my debt to that dear father for his early lessons in science; lessons which familiarized me as a child with scientific modes of thought and expression; laying a firm foundation, upon which a superstructure of further study could so easily be reared. It was he who first awoke my interest in such subjects; he who made Astronomy a living force in my imagination.

The teaching must have begun very early, for I well remember standing by his side, one wintry day, when I was certainly not more than seven or eight years old, asking why and how it could be that we were nearer to the Sun in winter than in summer, and yet were colder. A fire was burning, and he sat not far off. I can see now his fine, stately figure, the short-frocked child standing *by* his side, and the gesture with which he pointed to a fly on his knee. "See — if that fly were *one* inch nearer to the fire, would it feel any hotter?"

No; it would not. I understood that instantly; and though the real cause of summer and winter in the slant of Earth's axis did not become evident until long after, I did see then, with daylight clearness, that the difference of three million miles, compared with the Sun's whole distance, was no more than that one inch in the fly's distance from the fire. There was no need to ask more.

> "Heaven's ebon vault,
> Studded with stars unutterably bright,
> Thro' which the moon's unclouded grandeur rolls,
> Seems like a canopy which love has spread
> To curtain her sleeping world."
>
> P. B. SHELLEY.

PART II

STUDYING THE HEAVENS

I. - GROUPS OF STARS

LIKE every study, that of Astronomy has to be from small beginnings. To start with a difficult textbook or with hard calculations would, in most cases, have no good result.

It is a study which ought to be followed on two lines at the same time. Much can be learnt from books; much also from actual observation of the sky. A beginner may choose one plan or the other; but the better mode is to use both plans.

Without books, a student of the skies stands in much the same position as an ancient astronomer of Chaldean days. He has to find out for himself those things which have taxed the minds of men through centuries. And without some amount of watching of the heavens, the known facts which may be learnt from books can never be quite so real to him if he does not use his own eyes to verify them, to the small extent which lies in his power.

Some teachers of astronomy prefer to start with the distant stars and work their way back to such heavenly bodies as lie nearer to Earth. Others think it wise to tackle first the nearer bodies and gradually wander farther afield. For instance, we may begin with our closest neighbour of all, the Moon, and with our brother and sister worlds, the planets, and with the great head and center of our system, the Sun; afterwards passing on to the stars.

But even from the first, we cannot ignore the stars. Night by night, unless hidden by clouds, they shine forth; and from childhood, those tiny glimmers are a part of our lives.

With them, the earliest stage should be just to grow used to their ordinary look as seen from our Earth; to learn something of the various groups or "constellations"; to become acquainted with the shapes and names of such constellations and their places in the heavens; also to understand a little about their seeming nightly and yearly movements due to our own daily and yearly revolvings. What they really are, and how far they truly and actually move, must come later.

Earth's daily whirl on her own axis has been explained as making all the sky seem to travel round us by day and by night. And her yearly journey around the Sun also causes a slow shifting — apparent, not real — of the various constellations through summer and winter.

Certain constellations far north, such as the Great Bear and the Little Bear, are always visible to us in Great Britain and in the northern parts of Europe and North America. Certain constellations, such as the southern Cross, are never visible to us in those regions. But other constellations, not so far north and not so far south, are sometimes to be seen and sometimes not. Many stars high up in the southern sky — for instance, those in the constellation of Orion — visible to us in winter nights, are hidden in summer nights.

We can at any time see only those groups which lie in a direction *away from* the Sun; not those which lie on the same side of the heavens as the Sun. Those stars, if seen at all, would have to be seen by daylight; that is, at the same time as the Sun. And this, under ordinary conditions, is out of the question because they are veiled from our eyes by the glare of sunlight.

So, it is not until the Earth, in her twelve-month's voyage, gets around to the other side of the Sun and sees him against the opposite heavens, that the stars which were hidden months before become visible, while many stars that have been visible take their turn to disappear.

One fact should, from the first, be absolutely clear. This is *that the stars are always there*. They do not come and go. They are always overhead, high in the heavens, round the whole Earth, whether we see them or not.

I do not mean that the same stars are always over one particular part of the world, but that some stars are there always, which ones depending on which part of the heavens our part of the Earth happens to be under at any particular hour. The whole vast company of stars, each in its own constellation, to which it has belonged through thousands, if not millions, of years, is always in the skies.

If you had a good telescope, with a friend able to use it, you might get a glimpse of certain stars even in the brightest noonday.

Picture to yourself a small toy balloon floating in the air of a vast hall, with walls, ceiling, and floor, pictures and furniture surrounding it above, below, and on all sides. So, our Earth floats in the measureless expanse of space, with countless stars above, below, and on all sides.

Think of a small spider clinging to that little balloon. He would be able to see only part of the hall, whichever part towards which his side of the balloon happened to face. If he were looking at the right wall, he could not see the left, because the balloon between would hide it. And just so, we on Earth can, at any particular time, see only that part of the heavens towards which our side of this floating globe is turned.

Longfellow wrote on the subject -

> "And as the evening twilight fades away,
> The sky is filled with stars, invisible by day."

And Wordsworth:

> "Look for the stars, you'll say that there are none;
> Look up a second time, and one by one
> You mark them twinkling out with silvery light,
> And wonder how they could elude the sight."

The above illustration of the balloon and hall is, of course, defective, as such illustrations are bound to be. On Earth, we know no true "up" or "down," except in the sense of towards and away from our Earth's center. This is just as true in Australia as in Britain, even though the feet of our fellow subjects there do point towards the feet of men walking on British soil here.

Picture once again the small globe floating in the great hall, about halfway between floor and ceiling. But now think of it as obeying rule, as floating around and around a center occupied by another, much larger ball. Picture also that a slender needle is thrust through the little balloon's center, one end coming out at its north pole, the other at its south pole. And as it moves, that needle is slanting, not upright, and the slant is always in the same direction. The needle does not wobble about, pointing this way and that way; it points always steadily towards the same wall.

So, the axis of our Earth keeps always the same slant, and our north pole points always towards one part of the heavens. There lies the celestial north pole, carried straight on from the north pole of our little world.

In this slant of our Earth's axis lies the explanation of our seasons.

For in one part of our yearly journey around the Sun, our north pole points *towards* the Sun, and our south pole is turned *away* from him. This means the northern summer and the southern winter. Six months later, it is the south pole which points towards the Sun, and the north pole which is turned away from him. And though during that northern winter, we are really nearer to the Sun than in our summer, the trifling difference of three million miles is of little account. The main fact is that we have so much less actual direct sunshine, and that it comes to us from a Sun far lower down in the sky.

Spring and autumn lie between these two extremes, when the Earth is in a halfway position.

II. - HOW TO KNOW THE STARS

It is a good plan to cultivate the habit of looking from some particular window at certain stated hours after dusk each evening. Much may be learned thus. The brighter stars should first be picked out and carefully watched. It may be noted how they are placed with respect to neighboring stars not quite so bright; whether they twinkle or shine steadily; whether they keep, night after night, at the same distance from those other stars, or whether they slowly alter their positions; and if they do move, how they move.

This is one of the first questions of interest because thereby one may distinguish between stars and planets. A star twinkles; a planet generally does not. A star keeps always the same position among other stars; a planet wanders from one place to another among the stars.

Many years ago, a working man wrote to my father, begging for help in his efforts to learn about the heavenly bodies. In his letter, he made this remark: *"If I can once get hold of Venus, I will not let her go."*

No better plan could be suggested. Try to "get hold" of a planet here, of a star there, and do not let them go; do not lose them, but follow their movements day by day.

Bad weather may interrupt and confuse such attempts, and for a while, your new friends may slip out of sight, but they can be found again. They never really take their departure; they only change their positions.

The stars only change theirs in appearance, though in more ways than one. The planets change theirs, not only in appearance but also in reality, yet they always move by rule, and astronomers know at all times where to look for them.

Such watching as this means the giving of time and trouble, but it is worthwhile. Even while we must all depend largely on what others can tell us, since there is an enormous amount we could never discover for ourselves, yet the little we can do well repays for the effort.

In a sense, stars are more easily followed than planets, because through centuries they do not visibly alter their positions, one with regard to another. The different groups or constellations still look the same to us as they did in the days of the patriarchs. The soft shining of the Pleiades and the armor of Orion we see just as Job saw them. The Great Bear has not appreciably altered in shape since the time of Julius Caesar.

Even before learning the names of the constellations, you might become familiar with some of their shapes, and then, with the help of a star map, you could discover what they are called.

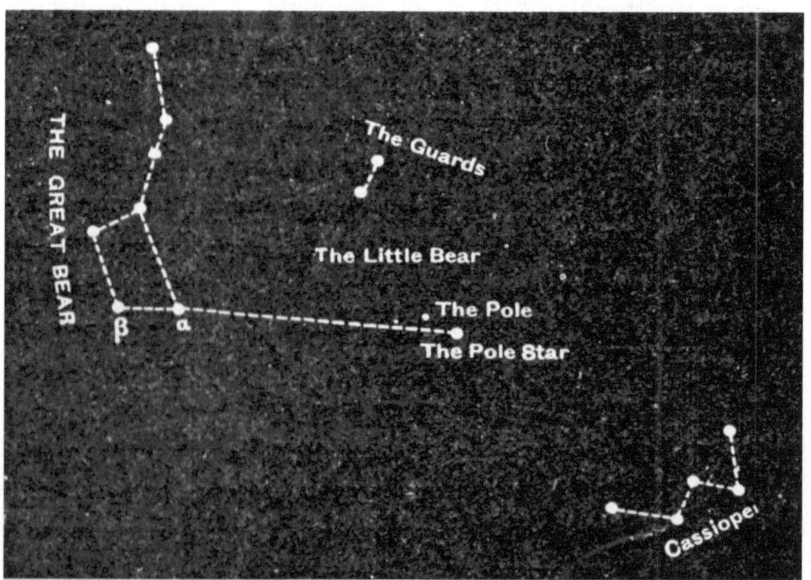

THE GREAT BEAR, POINTERS, AND POLE STAR

Or again, the map may be studied first, and afterward, you can try to find out the constellations and the chief stars belonging to them.

Though we speak of star magnitudes, which means star sizes, no true star in the sky can show any difference of size to us. The only real difference lies in degrees of brightness. A star of the first magnitude does not mean a star that looks bigger, but only a star that looks brighter. The light of each star comes in a single slender ray, and the star itself appears only as a *point* — even in the most powerful telescopes, it remains just a point! No telescope has yet been able to show a *disc* — a surface with measurable breadth — of any single star. Planets, on the other hand, do show discs that can be measured, but stars do not; they are simply too far away.

One of the first stars to be pointed out should be the Pole Star, at the tip of the Little Bear's tail. The two pointers of the Great Bear point toward the Pole Star. In the apparent daily whirl of the heavens, that faint Pole Star, located over our north pole, remains nearly stationary, while the constellations nearby circle around it, as seen from the northern hemisphere. This circling is not real; it is due to Earth's own daily rotation on its axis.

So Caesar claimed:

> "But I am constant as the Northern Star,
> Of whose true-fixed and resting quality
> There is no fellow in the firmament."[1]

Among those northern circling groups is the beautiful star Capella, in the constellation of Auriga, one of the brightest in our sky. Another glorious star, farther off, is Arcturus in Boötes. Other bright stars include Vega and Aldebaran.

The most radiant star in the entire sky is Sirius, which can only be seen in the winter months. Once you have located the magnificent constellation of Orion — also a winter constellation in the north — you can find Sirius with ease, as the two foot stars of Orion point in an almost straight line to this brilliant star with its diamond-like sparkle. On the other side of Sirius, you can spot the soft shimmer of

1   Shakespeare, *Julius Caesar*

the Pleiades, a cluster of dim stars appearing close together, although most observers can only distinguish six or seven. Nearby is another bright star, Aldebaran.[2]

The word "constellation" is from two Latin words which mean "star" and "together," or "connection." so the strict sense seems to be " a group of stars connected together." How far such stars really are connected is another question. Sometimes undoubtedly they are, but not always, and not necessarily.

This grouping of stars into definite constellations, with names, belongs to a very early period in the world's history.

> "Down steps Orion to the west,
>   High-headed, starry-eyed,
> Watchful beneath his warrior-crest,
>   His sword upon his side.
>
> "Amid the unnumbered stars of night
>   He fills his measured space,
> And covers under points of light
>   The fashion of his face.
>
> "He makes no gesture, gives no sign;
>   Yon form is all we know.
> So belt and scabbard used to shine
>   Millions of years ago.
>
> "Upon his brow endures no frown,
>   No tumult stirs his breast;
> In martial stride he still goes down
>   With all his stars at rest.
>
> "When Earth was young and Night was old,
>   That harness he put on,
> And girt for war, with nails of gold,
>   The belted warrior shone."[3]

2   In such studies of the heavens, great help may be obtained from a volume of star-maps, *Half-Hours with the Stars*, by R. A. Proctor. Their positions at different times and different hours are clearly given, with directions how to use the maps,
3   From *The Heart of Peace and Other Poems*, by Laurence Housman. Pub.: William Heinemann. By permission.

III. - SOME OTHER WORLDS

The planets in our Solar System — those in the Sun's family — are much closer to us than any star. They can be seen to move in the course of weeks and months. This movement is real, not just an illusion caused by our own movement. Planets journey around the Sun, just as Earth does, and appear to move among the "fixed stars."

Actually, they do nothing of the kind. What happens is that, in their onward movements, we see them *against* one star-group after another in the sky. It is much the same as if you stood on the beach, watching a small boat some little distance out. You would see it against one far-off ship after another, as it passed along; and this would not mean that the boat ever went near those ships, but only that you happen to see the two in the same "line of sight," though they might be separated by many miles of water.

Again, no stars are truly" fixed," though by reason of their enormous distance they seem to us to be so, keeping their constellation-shapes unchanged through centuries.

Most easily found and most easily kept of all the planets is Venus, the lovely "Evening Star" of some months in the year, and quite as truly the "Morning Star" of other months. Venus is not a star at all, but a planet or world, much the same in size as this world on which we live. No other planet and no star in all the sky shines with such a lustre as Venus at her best; not because she is larger or brighter than all other heavenly bodies, but because she is better placed for our powers of sight.

Once get this beautiful orb pointed out to you, and you may enjoy her soft resplendence evening after evening, or morning after morning, weather permitting. She is never very far away from the Sun, being nearer to him than we are ourselves. You will always find her, when she is visible, either in the western sky soon after sunset, or else in the eastern sky a little while before sunrise.

Mercury may be seen in the same manner; but as this small world is still closer to the Sun than Venus, he is much oftener lost in the Sun's radiance. At the best of times he is less easy to find, because he is so small, and also because he rises such a short time before the Sun, and sets such a short time after him.

Next to Venus in brightness, as seen by us, comes Jupiter, often a most beautiful sight. When you notice a particularly bright body, not twinkling like a star, but shining with a strong and steadfast light, in a part of the sky where Venus cannot be because it is too distant

COMPARATIVE SIZES OF JUPITER AND EARTH

from the rising or setting Sun, you may feel pretty sure that you are gazing on Jupiter.

The pathway of Jupiter round the Sun, unlike that of Venus, is a great deal farther away than our own. You should go to an almanac for news as to his whereabouts in any special month, since he can be seen in many parts of the sky, though, as said above, he may often be recognised simply by his brilliance. And when you have found him, you may follow his movements too by night, for a good while if the weather permits.

Mars also may be seen in various parts of the sky; for the pathway of Mars, like that of Jupiter, lies outside the pathway of Earth.

Quite a small world is this interesting little globe, much smaller than Earth, though not so small as Mercury. He is one of our nearest celestial friends, while Jupiter - decisively the biggest member of the Sun's family - lies far away.

Saturn, the next in size after Jupiter, a most lovely and marvellous world, is so very distant, and in consequence is often so very dim, that he may be less easily found by a beginner. The two outer planets, Uranus and Neptune, can only be seen with the help of a telescope.

Of all these brother and sister worlds, none perhaps has awakened keener interest with people generally than Mars. At one time much popular talk went on about the possibilities of intercourse with Martian people supposing that any such people exist. "Flag-wagging" had even been suggested as a mode of interchanging ideas - till one authority stated that a flag, to be seen there, would have to be about the size of Ireland!

PART III

THE SILVER MOON

I. - OUR PLACID COMPANION

ALL the world knows her, round-faced and calm, serene and distant, yet faithful in comradeship. She never wanders very far away. She never seeks another fellow-traveller.

We may count securely upon her, for she is regular in her habits, and is sure to be in those parts of our sky where she is expected by those who understand her ways. If, at such times, we fail to see her, that is the result of earthly mists which rise between; not *her* fault.

To be sure, she does not shine at one and the same hour upon all parts of this round globe. Manifestly, it would be impossible. When she is on one side of the solid Earth, she cannot be on the other side also. And when she happens to be in the same part of the sky as the Sun, her light is smothered by his greater radiance. But still, she goes on, travelling around and with her big companion, keeping always over a certain belt of Earth's surface, within a definite distance north or south of the equator.

And if she is sometimes large and bright, and sometimes only a narrow sickle of light, that, again, is not her fault. She cannot shine except on the side which is turned towards the Sun and reflects his brightness, since she has no light whatever of her own. If that side which faces the Sun is turned partly away from Earth, we see only a portion of it—half-Moon, or quarter-Moon, or a mere slender bow, as the case may be. And when it is turned wholly away, as at New Moon, we see nothing of her.

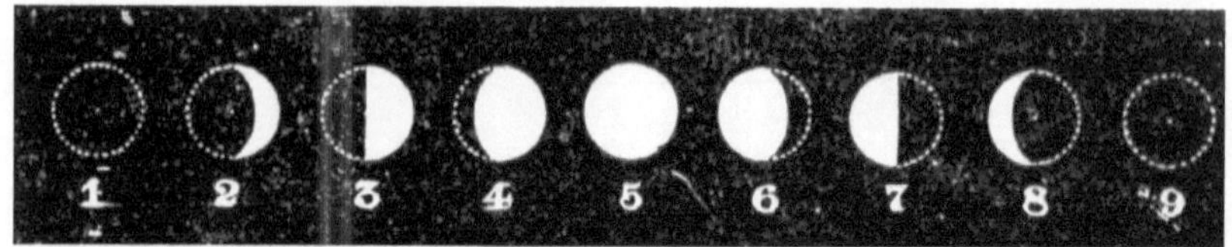

PHASES OF THE MOON

These changes are called "phases," and perhaps you know Jean Ingelow's lines, as supposed to be spoken by a child of seven -

> "O Moon, in the night I have seen you sailing
>   And shining, so round and low;
> You were bright, ah, bright; but your light is failing —
>   You are nothing now but a bow."
>
> You Moon, have you done something wrong in Heaven,
>   That God has hidden your face?
> I hope, if you have, you will soon be forgiven,
>   And shine again in your place."

For a little child now, as for a grown man of ancient days with complete ignorance of astronomy, no reasons exist, or did exist, *why* the round Moon should thus alter her shape, week after week, month after month.

Have you ever seen a piece of magnesium-wire set alight in a dark room? If so, you may have noticed two things — first, the dazzling brilliance of the burning wire; second, the lesser brightness of all around, including people's faces. That burning wire shone, as the Sun shines, by its own radiant light. But the faces and walls and ceiling shone as the Moon shines, by a reflection of the light given to them.

Half of the Moon shines always in the blaze of sunlight poured upon it; but not the whole of that half can always be seen by us. And this, as already said, is why we often see a mere crescent of light — not because the Moon has a less bright face than usual, but because most of that face is turned away, so that we only catch a glimpse of one edge of its brightness.

Still, we must remember that all the while the whole round Moon is *there*, a solid globe, half-bright, half-dark.

A friend[4] once sent me a Christmas card and wrote with it: "Two stars, actually, in the Moon! Times can't be improving, as we are so fond of imagining; for Coleridge only spoke of 'one bright star' within the horned Moon's 'nether tip'; and now, in 1884, someone was found capable of putting two stars in the Moon!"

The artist who designed the said card, having sketched a crescent-Moon in the sky, proceeded to place a couple of stars *inside the crescent*. He utterly forgot that the crescent-shape is filled with the solid dark body of the Moon. A star might lie just in that direction, far, far away beyond the Moon, but no one on Earth could see it because the Moon would lie between. *And no star in all the Universe ever comes between the Moon and the Earth.*

Occasionally we can see for ourselves that the dark body is there. It only happens now and then, but it does happen. The bright Moon-face, lit up by the Sun, is chiefly turned away, so that we have no more than a sickle of light. But the dark Moon-face, which is towards us, catches a gleam from the shining of our Earth. Then we can see faintly the dark body of the Moon inside the bright crescent, and we call it "the Old Moon in the arms of the New."

But the New Moon and the Old Moon are the same Moon.

Perhaps the idea of our Earth shining may be new to you. Yet she does shine. She is just as much a "heavenly body" as the Moon is, and as any planet is. Like them, she shines by borrowed light, reflected from the Sun.

If we could see our dull old Earth, as she sometimes may be seen from Venus, for example, we should be amazed at her radiant beauty. We should not wonder then that the Moon can sometimes borrow some of our brightness.

In her night-journey, as she seems to travel across the sky, she comes between the stars and us, blotting out one star after another. At the time of full-Moon, very few can be visible in her near neighbourhood, because of her shining. But when she becomes a mere sickle of light, something else can be observed, which proves the actual presence of the dark body.

4   Lady Huggins, wife of the great spectroscopist.

Watch carefully for a bright star disappearing behind that outer shining Moon-edge. You will not see it when quite close to the rounded sickle-edge, but you may notice the Moon's drawing near, till it vanishes. Then you can watch for the reappearance of the same star on the other side — the inner side.

But you will not see it directly the sickle of light has passed. You will not detect it anywhere *within* the rim of brightness, for that rim holds the solid body of the Moon. And the star cannot appear again till the whole Moon, both the bright rim and the dark body, has passed by. Then it will once more be visible, not close to the crescent, but beyond the dark Moon-body.

Through countless ages, the Moon has been *our* Moon. Not Jupiter's Moon, nor Mars' Moon, nor Saturn's Moon; but Earth's own particular possession. No world in the whole Solar System, so far as we know, gets any good out of the Moon except this Earth. She is not even the Sun's Moon, in any especial sense, beyond the fact that the Moon, like the Earth, is one of his planets, a very small one.

We often speak of Sun and Moon together because, for us, the one is king of day, the other is queen of night. The Moon is to us what she can be to no other heavenly body in the Universe. But the Sun is to all his planets, in a greater or less degree, what he is to us. And though we could, so far as light and heat are concerned, manage to exist without the Moon, it is far otherwise with regard to the Sun. Apart from him, our world would speedily become one vast tomb of death.

Early in the last century, a popular song was afloat offering a comparison between the two from an extremely Irish point of view. It began as follows -

> "Och, long life to the Moon for a swate noble cratur,
> That serves us for lamplight each night in the dark;
> While the Sun only shines in the day, which by nature
> Needs no light at all, as you all may remark.
> But as for the Moon, sir, I will be bound, sir,
> 'Twould save the whole nation a great many pound, sir,
> To subscribe for to light her up all the year round, sir."

A difficult feat, this last, for even an Irishman to carry through; while if once that great luminary, the Sun, were blotted out, it would soon be seen how little brightness "day" could boast "by nature."

The Sun once gone, all warmth, all life, all growth, would be at an end, and the only light remaining would be that of the dim and twinkling stars. No Moon or planets would then be seen, no bright Venus or Jupiter could gladden our sky; for there would be no Sun to lend them of his brilliance. Even if certain of the planets have some faint power to shine of themselves, it would be too feeble a glimmer to benefit our Earth.

II. - IN STRONG CONTRAST

The Moon is a globe, in shape much like this world, but not nearly so large.

A piece of tape, just long enough to be passed straight through the Earth's centre, reaching from one side to the other, would serve to measure the Moon in two ways. One quarter of the tape might be passed in the same manner through the Moon's centre, the two ends

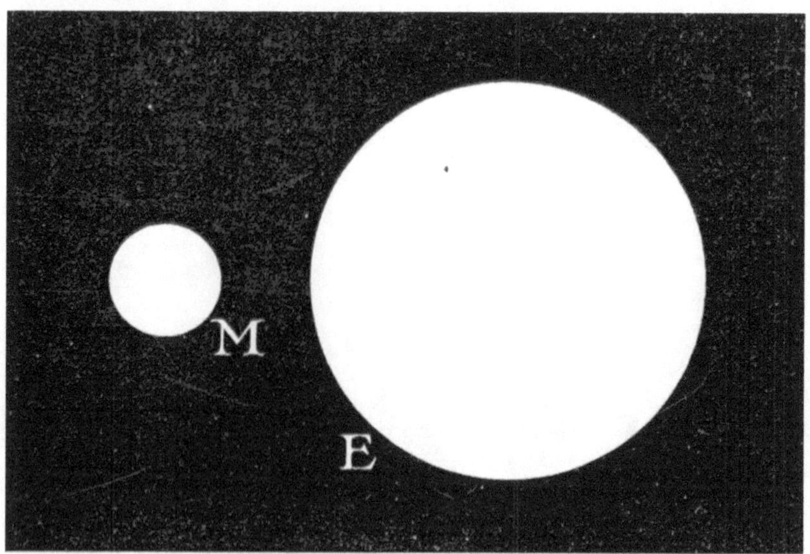

DIAMETER, 2163 MILES. DIAMETER, 7912 MILES.

COMPARATIVE SIZES OF EARTH AND MOON

just touching her opposite sides; and the remaining three-quarters could be folded round the Moon's equator, with the two ends meeting.

That gives some idea of the *comparative* sizes of the two. You might find a couple of balls, the *through-measure* of the one just serving for the two measurements of the other. Then you would see this comparison more clearly.

If you wanted to make, out of several Moons, each the size of our Moon, a single globe as large as the Earth, you would need for that purpose nearly fifty Moons. But if, in the same way, you wished to make a globe as large as the Sun, you would need well over fifty million of Moons.

Such a tape, just long enough to be passed through the Moon from side to side, would have to be two thousand miles long. But a tape

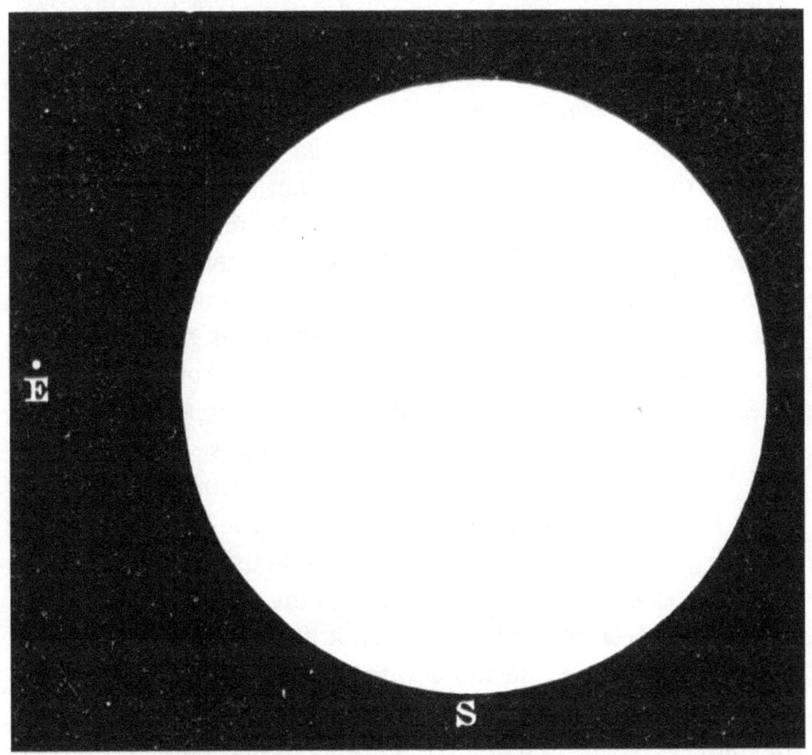

COMPARATIVE SIZES OF SUN AND EARTH

which could be passed through the Sun, from side to side, would have to be nearly nine hundred thousand miles long! Rather a difference!

As a mere matter of guesswork, nobody would ever imagine, looking first at the one and then at the other, that the Sun is so huge compared with the Moon. And for ages in the world's history, nobody did imagine it.

So long as the two were supposed to be just about the same distance away, it was impossible that their sizes could be known. Until telescopes were made, and many other astronomical instruments had been invented, until also countless improvements had come about both in telescopes and in other instruments, the measurement of heavenly bodies was out of the question.

If the Sun really were, as used to be thought, just as near to us as the Moon, he would be an appalling object. Not alone from his colossal size, but because of the ocean of furious fiery gases which enfold his whole surface, and because of the fierce and whirling storms, the fearful heat, the scorching glare.

Could such an event come to pass, as that the Sun should approach to where the Moon now is, then at any instant, vast tongues of glowing hydrogen gas — great crimson "flames" — might leap from the Sun and enwrap our little Earth in their fervid embrace. Such mighty outbursts are no rare matter on the Sun, sometimes reaching to a height of more than three hundred thousand miles. And the Moon is only two hundred and forty thousand miles away from us.

But that the Earth should remain in her present position, moving still at her present speed, under such circumstances, would be impossible. So terrific would be the force of the Sun's attraction that, long before he could draw thus near, she would have leapt with lightning speed to greet him, and would have been lost in that fierce tumultuous sea of fire, as a pebble drops and is lost in the ocean.

While therefore we may be thankful for the light and heat bestowed upon us by the Sun — without which we could not live — we may also be thankful that he is placed at a safe distance. We may congratulate ourselves that it is not the raging and storm-driven Sun, but the cold and quiet Moon which lies only a few thousand miles away; even though the poet Tennyson did look upon her as a rather unsympathetic friend, when he wrote —

> "Oh, a cold, cold glance hath the Lady Moon,
>   And a stately step, and slow,
>   As with queenly gaze, so proud and pure,
>   She looketh on all below.
>
> "She pauseth not on her onward path,
>   To list to the mourner's sigh;
>   She pitieth not the throbbing pulse,
>   Nor the dim and sunken eye."

Still, if somewhat impassive, she is constant in her attachment. And it is better to depend on her steadfast shining than to have only the will-o'-the-wisp flash of a shooting star, or the uncertain visits of a comet. We do at least know when we may expect her; and she never fails to arrive punctually to the minute.

It is fair, however, to add that Shakespeare did not, through the voice of one of his characters, allow her even the virtue of steadfastness —

> "O swear not by the Moon, the unconstant Moon,
>   (That monthly changes in her circled orb)
>   Lest that thy love prove likewise variable."[5]

So though the Sun and Moon fill much the same space in our sky, this does not mean that they are the same in bulk. Far from it! The Sun is enormously the larger of the two, and also he is immensely farther off. To the latter fact is due their seeming likeness in size. The very much greater distance lessens hugely his apparent — not his real — size. A man who is fifty or a hundred yards away may look to our sight much bigger than a house which is half a mile or a mile away, yet that does not make him as large as the house.

Our Moon's distance from us is not always exactly the same. She travels round in a pathway, or orbit, which may be described as slightly oval in shape, and the Earth is not at the precise centre of that oval. In

5   Shakespeare: *Romeo and Juliet.*

one part of her monthly tour, she is more than twenty-six thousand miles nearer to Earth than in another part. The two hundred and forty thousand miles which—speaking roughly—separate her from Earth, though a good deal when compared with distances on Earth itself, form a very insignificant little gap when compared with the wider heavenly distances which separate star from star.

III. - SIZES AND DISTANCES

Before saying more about the Queen of Night, it may be well to pause and try to give a general notion of the sizes of a few leading members of our Solar System, and of the distances separating them one from another.

A train has been already imagined as going steadily at the rate of fifty miles an hour, never slackening or pausing night or day, travelling direct from one side of our Earth to the other, straight through the centre. Such a train, starting perhaps in the neighbourhood of the British Isles, and coming out in the neighbourhood of Australia, might accomplish its journey in less than a week. The same train, always at the same speed, with no stoppages, may be pictured as making the following journeys —

Round the whole Earth, on the equator, in nearly three weeks.

Through the centre of the Moon, from one side to the other, in about two days.

Round the whole Moon, on the Moon's equator, in about six days.

Through the centre of the Sun, from one side to the other, in nearly two years.

Round the whole Sun, on the Sun's equator, in something under six years.

If you master these simple figures, you will gain a fairly clear idea of the *relative* sizes of Earth, Moon, and Sun.

Then about the distances of certain planets from ourselves — of

Venus, Mars, and Jupiter — the most easily seen in our sky. With them, we will take the *nearest* positions. Each planet is sometimes on the same side of the Sun as our Earth, and at certain dates, each one comes into a direct line with both Earth and Sun. That is the very closest point to which each planet draws. At other times, each may be very far away, right off on the other side of the Sun, and then the dividing gap is immensely increased.

It may help you to gain an idea of how this comes about if you place on the floor a small ball, then drop round it, lying flat, a small hoop. Round that lay a second and bigger hoop; round that a third, still larger; and round that a fourth, much larger still. The ball in the centre is the Sun; the smallest of the hoops is the pathway of Venus round the Sun; the next is the pathway of our Earth; then comes the pathway of Mars, and lastly, you have the pathway of Jupiter. Other planets, nearer or farther than these, we are leaving alone for the present.

Suppose that a very tiny ball is journeying round and round each hoop, moving at different speeds. Those nearer to the central ball go faster; those farther out go more slowly. So sometimes one on one hoop overtakes another on the next hoop, or lags behind it. Sometimes two are quite near together, and sometimes they are on opposite sides of the little ball which lies between them. That is how the planets travel round the Sun.

Only there are many more of them than those three, and the pathways, or orbits, are not round, but slightly oval, and the distances between those various pathways are wide.

Each one of these chief planets keeps always to its own orbit. Not one of them ever invades the orbit of another. Venus never gets near to the Earth's orbit from one side, and Mars never approaches it from the other.

Now imagine the same train as before, always at the same unchanging speed, making the following trips —

Straight from the Earth to the Moon in less than seven months.

Straight from the Earth to the Sun in about two hundred and ten years. See what a contrast there is between the space which separates

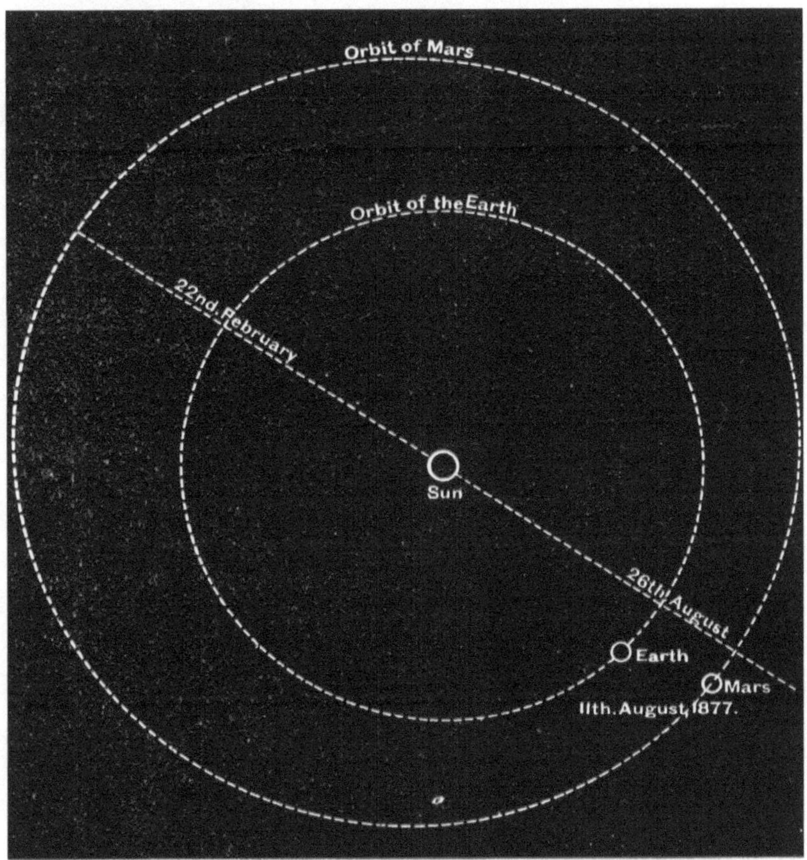

THE EARTH AND MARS WHEN AT THEIR NEAREST POSITIONS

the Moon from Earth, and that which separates Earth and Sun. Next come certain planets.

Straight from Earth to the planet Venus, when the two are at their very nearest points, in rather less than sixty years.

Straight from Earth to the planet Mars, when at their nearest, in somewhere about eighty years.

And straight from Earth to the huge planet Jupiter, once more when at their nearest, in about eight hundred and thirty years.

You see how much nearer we are to the Sun than to outlying

members of his family. And Jupiter is the closest of all the four great outer worlds.

These are the lesser gaps, dividing our Earth from her brother and sister planets. When she is on one side of the Sun, and a planet is on the further side, the gaps widen enormously.

The planet-pathways, thus described, and all the other planet-orbits in our Solar System, lie in very much the same *plane*. That is to say, they are placed in the heavens much as the hoops lie on the floor — tilted, indeed, a little, this way or that way, but keeping in the main nearly to one level, not slanting about in all sorts of directions.

PART IV

WHAT THE MOON IS REALLY LIKE

I. - AIR AND WATER

THE poet Wordsworth, speaking of the sky, puts one or two questions in his serious fashion -

> "Is nothing of that radiant pomp so good as we have here?
> Or gives a thing but small delight that never can be dear?
> The silver Moon, with all her vales and hills of mightiest fame
> Doth she betray us when they're seen? Or are they but a name?"

No, she does not "betray us," for they really are "hills and vales," or rather, mountains and ravines, of a sort; but different in kind from those of Earth. And it is not impossible that a great deal of "that radiant pomp" — if by the term we may understand the Universe as a whole — may be not only as good as, but a great deal better than aught that "we have here." But for the Moon, we can have no hesitation in answering with a decisive "No." Fair and bright though she looks, nobody need wish to exchange life on Earth for life on the Moon; at all events, while his spirit inhabits his present body.

So long as he must breathe earthly air to live, he could not exist there for ten minutes. Even if, by any mechanical means, that difficulty could at some future day be overcome, our sister-world would still be a very uncomfortable habitation.

Though the distance is a mere nothing compared with other celestial distances, very little could be known of her surface before the invention of telescopes. Just the brightness and the markings — the

49

round, complacent face, or the man with his bundle of sticks — and a few guesses whether these might represent lands and seas; and that was nearly all. But telescopes soon made a difference.

Not only could grey plains be clearly seen, but lofty mountains also; and great circular mountain ramparts and rings; and countless volcanic craters, some huge, some small, scattered lavishly about; and curious lighter streaks amid wide, dusky spaces.

As telescopes have been made with greater and greater powers, so our knowledge of the Moon has grown, especially in recent years with the added help of photography.

The question is sometimes asked — how near are we practically brought to the Moon by our largest telescopes? How much can we really see?

This is not merely a question of the largest telescopes. It is seldom that the highest powers can be used with advantage. If they could, we might speak of "bringing the Moon to a distance of a hundred, or even eighty miles." Actually, it can hardly be said that she can be clearly seen nearer than perhaps a hundred and twenty miles.

Even then, the distance, though a mere nothing from one point of view, means a good deal with regard to eyesight. If we think of one hundred and twenty miles side by side with — let us say — ten thousand miles, the space sinks into a mere speck; yet when we begin to consider how much and how little can be distinguished by the naked eye on Earth, at a distance of a hundred and twenty miles, matters wear another aspect.

However, photographs, taken with powerful telescopes and enlarged, do show us "structures" on the Moon not more than two or three miles in diameter. Craters of that size have been detected in numbers, which is not bad for a world two hundred and forty thousand miles away.

During many years, it was looked upon as certain that no air existed on the Moon. If any atmosphere in the least like our own were there, the Moon's outline could not be so sharp and clear. It would, and more especially when seen through a telescope, have a softened and blurred look. But this never happens.

So, practically, it is correct to say that our companion has not an atmosphere, though this does not forbid the possibility of a very, very thin and slight amount of air — so thin and slight that it would not support any animal life such as we know on Earth.

Once upon a time, our sister-globe may have had a more "substantial" atmosphere; but if so, it has all but vanished. She is so small in size that her power of attraction has probably been too feeble to hold her atmosphere captive. So gradually all or most of its particles have wandered far away, never to return.

Our Earth holds fast her ocean of air simply by the force of her attractive power; and here, seemingly, the Moon has failed, because she is so much smaller and lighter in make.

When the grey markings on the Moon's face were first examined through telescopes, they were seen to be broad spaces, bordered often by mountain ranges, and the idea naturally sprang up that they might be oceans, like our earthly oceans. But though they are still called "seas," no one now believes that they are actual oceans. Some astronomers have looked upon them as possible old sea-beds, from which the water has long since disappeared.

> "Then the Moon in all her pride,
> Like a spirit glorified,
> Filled and overflowed the night
> With revelations of her light."
>
> LONGFELLOW

II. - MOUNTAINS AND CRATERS

With the help of a small telescope, or even of a good binocular or field-glass, it is easy to see mountains and craters at the broken "edge" of brightness of a half-Moon, on a clear night. Some of the tiny tips stand out curiously, quite apart from the main body, because the lower mountain slopes are in shadow. It is just as, in Switzerland, one may see mountain summits glowing in sunshine, while the lower parts are deep in shadow.

At the same time, odd little bright circles may be noted. They are some of the great round mountain ramparts or crater-like formations which abound there. Though the Moon is so small a globe, she vies with Earth in the height of her ranges. She has her Alps and her Apennines — so named by earthly observers.

In those far-off Alps is another Mont Blanc; not so lofty as ours. But the lunar Apennines have no less than three thousand high peaks, all visible from here, and among those peaks are summits from fifteen to eighteen thousand feet high, not only equalling but outdoing our Mont Blanc.

Clefts and gorges are seen, and long, narrow channels, sometimes described as grooves or furrows, with high steep sides. And certain of the large craters are surrounded with bright streaks, radiating out in a curious star-like pattern.

Some astronomers believe these to be cracks in the Moon's crust,

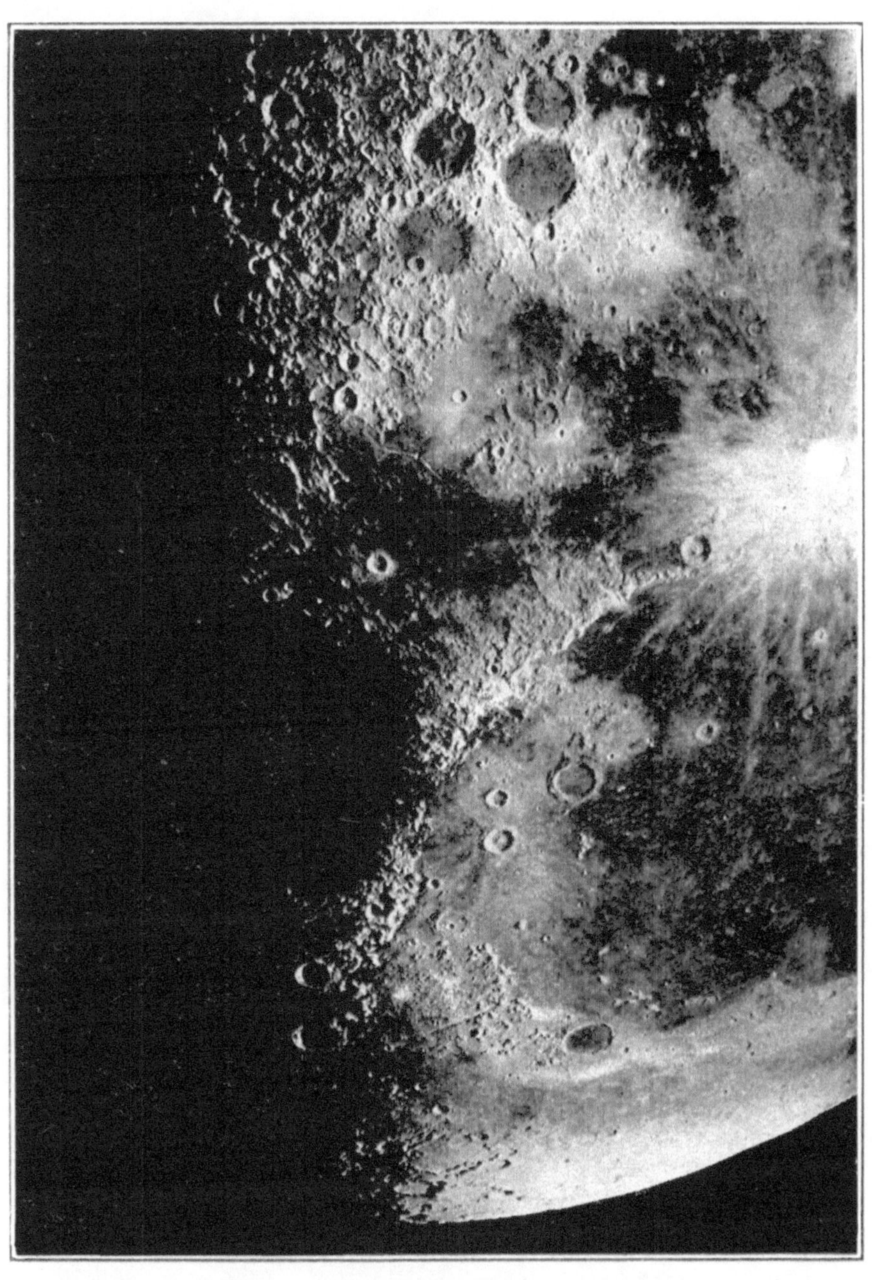

PORTION OF MOON, NORTH POLE TO AGRIPPA
PHOTOGRAPH BY G. E. HALE, OCT. 5, 1909

many of them hundreds of miles long. It has been suggested that the brightness *might* be due to deposits of salt — perhaps left there by former oceans — shining in the sunlight.

To an extraordinary degree, that bright surface is studded with craters. The larger ones may be as much as a hundred, or even a hundred and fifty miles across — real circular mountain ranges, generally enclosing more or less level plains, in the centre of which a solitary mountain sometimes rears its head. From these, all varieties of crater-like formations, down to little crater pits or crater cones under three miles in diameter, are lavishly strewn over the face of our satellite! She is indeed "pock-marked."

A well-known crater-like formation is "Copernicus," a circular mountain wall, fifty-six miles across and rising to thirteen thousand feet in height. It encloses a plain, which is broken by hills, some of which are as much as two thousand feet high; and many bright rays diverge from it.

The explanation was long widely held, and is still held in many quarters, that these craters, both large and small, are due mainly to volcanic action in the long past. But if so, the volcanoes now are silent and dead.

Another theory of explanation has been lately put forward, to some extent a revival of an old theory, once maintained and then given up. This is that the craters may be due, not to volcanic action, but to the crashing down of huge meteorites on the Moon's surface, in ages when that surface was soft and impressionable, and when enormous multitudes of such meteorites may have circled round the Sun, extending to the Moon's neighbourhood.

To some minds, the volcanic explanation may seem the easier of belief; at all events, as accounting for the larger craters.

We can no longer speak with unquestioning confidence of the condition of the Moon as absolutely "dead" — changeless — lifeless. Observations made during recent years have to a certain extent shaken this belief. Slight alterations of outline have been here or there noticed which, if real, might have been caused by something in the nature of falls of rock or landslides. And these may have been partly due to the tremendous variations of temperature. For during the Moon's long day and long night, changes from blazing heat to unspeakable cold, and from unspeakable cold to blazing heat, are said to range between some *four hundred and fifty degrees*; while we on Earth think much of a range of fifty or sixty degrees of temperature.

Another explanation given for these slight changes of outline seen at times is that they may have come about through the bombardment of the Moon's surface by exceptionally large and heavy meteorites. This too is at least a "may-be," though in the opinion of some eminent astronomers, it is not very likely.

Moreover, through long and careful watching from an observatory in Jamaica, many small and brilliant white spots have been seen on the summits of mountain ranges, and these have been regarded as perhaps snow. The Moon does not have ice-caps, like Mars, but such spots suggest the possibility of snow. Certain passing appearances also have been noticed, which the observer translated into probable snowstorms.

A difficulty comes in here, however. Both rain and snow with us are the result of the condensation of water vapour floating in our atmosphere. But the Moon, being so small a globe, has not, it is considered, enough attractive power to hold captive an atmosphere of water vapour; so it would seem that snowstorms there can hardly come into being. One authority, pointing this out, states that "the white spots would almost certainly slowly melt and evaporate in the sunlight," and that, if matters be thus, "it would mean that no gas lighter than carbon dioxide — carbonic acid gas — could be retained by the Moon," and that "this leaves open the possibility that the white spots are solid (frozen) carbon dioxide."

From that same cause, the small size of the Moon and the consequent very slight pressure of so thin an atmosphere, it is believed that water would boil at the freezing point; a curious state of things, with results which it is difficult for us fully to estimate.

Again, certain other appearances have been observed which are held by some astronomers to point to the problematic existence of vegetation — a very low order of it at best! We are told that this lunar vegetation is not green, but grey or purplish-black; which might suggest something in the nature of fungi.

One American astronomer[6], while upholding this "vegetation" view, carefully explains that the "form of any such growth is, of course, quite unknown to us, and the phenomena may consist merely in the darkening and fading of its exposed surface. As has been mentioned in previous articles, *we assume the phenomena to be due to vegetation, because that explanation is plausible, and because none other of any sort has ever been offered for it.*"

But other explanations may yet be forthcoming; and any such "assumed" interpretations should always be held lightly, pending further evidence and more definite proofs.

6   Prof. W. H. Pickering.

III. - DAY AND NIGHT

It becomes fairly evident that our nearest neighbour in the heavens would hardly do for a summer resort, even if we could manage somehow to cross safely the gulf of more than two hundred thousand airless miles lying between.

The Moon's daylight time is always on that part of her surface which faces the Sun; her time of darkness is always on that part which is turned away from the Sun.

This is with her as with us. But while our day, caused by Earth's whirl on her axis, lasts twenty-four hours — including hours both of light and of darkness — the Moon's day, caused also by her much slower whirl on her axis, lasts through four of our weeks or twenty-eight of our days. so the length of her "day" — taking together as one the hours of light and of darkness — is exactly the same as the time that she takes to travel once around our Earth. In consequence of this, she turns always one side to us, and never the opposite side.

Whether that side too is studded and pock-marked with countless craters, large and small, we may conjecture, but we cannot know. Not a single human being in this world has ever gazed on the further side of the Moon.

At Full Moon, we see the whole of her bright side, as illumined by the Sun, during its daytime. At New Moon, that bright side is turned away from us. But what we do see, either at the Full, or before and after the New, is *always the same side*. Invariably we have the same mountains and plains, taking shape as an old man gathering sticks, or as a comic human face, never changing.

Think what the contrast must be, between the fortnight of burning, glaring heat — unsoftened by any atmosphere worth mentioning — lasting unbroken through two weeks or so of Earth-time — and the black darkness, the awful icy chill, of the next two weeks, with no air to capture and keep any of the Sun's warmth. The cold then must be simply appalling.

And even in the long day of blazing heat, though in direct sunshine the thermometer might rise to any extent, yet the climate must be similar to that of our loftiest mountain tops, where hard freezing goes on side by side with considerable heat. Far more so, indeed, on the Moon, where practically no air exists. The slightest shade, cutting off direct heat, would mean at once overwhelming cold.

One beautiful sight may be seen from the Moon — if any beings were there to enjoy it! — and that is the Earth in the Moon's sky, a splendid globe, more than a dozen times as large as the Moon in our sky, and gloriously bright. But only on part of the Moon can this wonderful vision appear — that side which invariably faces us, and from which Earth is visible as a fixed globe, steadily turning round and round, but always at a single spot in the heavens. The other unfortunate side of our satellite has no such help in its long winter nights. Stars and planets alone can be seen from there.

Though the Moon may possibly have come into being later than the Earth, she is really the older of the two. Age is not a question of years alone. Even with human beings, we sometimes see a man of sixty-five who is younger than another of fifty-five, and it is the same with heavenly bodies. Earth still enjoys a hale and vigorous middle age, while the Moon is aged and decrepit. She has passed through youth and middle age, and has reached old age, much faster than our Earth, because of the greater size of the latter. A small globe will always cool down faster than a large one of the same make. And this is very much a matter of cooling down. You will hear more about it in connection with other worlds.

We need not believe that she has always been what she seems to be in the present. But if she was once alive as our Earth is alive, that is over. No fiery volcanoes pour forth molten matter. No changeful clouds float in her sky. She is of use to us in many ways, but we cannot imagine that she is of use to living creatures on her surface. Animal life, in any form known to us, could hardly exist on such a world now, whatever may have been in the long past.

Somebody may ask how we can speak with any sort of confidence about the past of our Moon or of other worlds in the sky. And, of course, in many respects, we cannot be sure. No human being was there in these far-back ages to see how the worlds came into being — in what manner they were "framed" by the Divine Creator. Yet in one sense, we have reasons for a certain amount of confidence.

If in the woodlands you come across an old, dead, withered tree trunk, you are absolutely convinced that this aged trunk was once upon a time a living and growing tree. So, too, in God's wondrous Garden of the Skies, when we find what seems to be an aged and used-up world, we can feel little doubt that, once upon a time, and at least to some extent, that world may have been warm and living and useful. Both here and in the heavens, things become old and used-up in the course of time.

But though in certain respects the Moon may be described as used-up, she cannot be called useless. We on Earth know well her value. As a mirror catching and giving forth again the rays of sunlight, she serves us often for a night lamp. And if it were not for the steady, ceaseless power of her attraction, as exerted on ocean waters, the whole system of tides throughout the world would be different from what it now is — with consequences which we can hardly calculate.

> "Then out of the east in a paling mist,
> The dead-faced Moon came up to be kissed;
> Slow and solemn, we watched her rise,
> A face of wonder with cavernous eyes.
> There life is changeless, and time without worth,
> There nothing dies or is brought to birth;
> Her day is done, she is filled with dearth;
> Old she looks to the young green Earth,

Old as the foam of a frozen shore,
Old — for nothing can age her more.

"O young green Earth, go down into night,
Rejoice in thy youth, till its days are o'er;
Time speeds, life spends; therein is delight
Till youth and the years can age no more."[7]

7   From *The Heart of Peace and Other Poems* by Laurence Housman, Pub.: William Heinemann, by permission.

PART V

THE FAIR WORLD
VENUS

I. - COOLING BODIES

WE will turn now from the thought of our very near neighbour to another bright world in the sky, belonging to the family of our Sun — beautiful Venus.

It should at the outset be fully grasped that when "bright worlds in the sky" are spoken about, stars are *not* meant. Those countless twinkling specks of light, which night by night spangle the heavens, are not "worlds."

True, a star may conceivably be on the road to becoming a world. But that road is very long, and the goal may lie at an enormous distance ahead.

Each separate star which we can see is, in all likelihood, a brilliant sun, larger or smaller, brighter or fainter, than our Sun, clothed like him in an ocean of fiercely raging gases, shining like him with its own terrific heat.

Also, each separate star is, in all probability, parting with its abundant stores of heat; and unless by some means those lost stores can be replaced, it must become, in the far distant future, a cooled and therefore a non-shining body. When so cooled, and not before, it may possibly deserve to be classed as a "world," instead of as a sun. On the other hand, it may be only a "dark sun," and such dark suns are believed to be many in number, scattered widely through the skies, like derelict ships on the ocean.

Whether it can then possess any brightness will depend on whether it is near enough to any radiant sun to reflect the rays of the latter. If it can do this, it will still be too dim to be visible to us from so great a distance.

And even then, if it does catch and cast forth such light, unless it actually belongs to that radiant sun — unless it is controlled and warmed and lighted by him — it could hardly be called in the usual sense "a world."

No world in the sky, properly so named, shines to any very marked extent by reason of its own intrinsic brightness, but mainly at least, if not entirely, by reason of the light of its sun, through borrowed radiance.

Venus, Mars, and Mercury would not be bright worlds at all, but only dark bodies, invisible here, if they were not clothed in the Sun's rays. Jupiter might indeed be dimly visible, and Saturn very much more dimly, since these great planets are now believed to give forth some amount of light, though a very much smaller amount than what they show to us. And other worlds in the Universe, belonging to other suns, which we may be pretty confident do exist — albeit we cannot see them — would probably be in the same condition.

A "world" in the language of Astronomy does not of necessity mean one in which people live, or even one which is in a fit state to be inhabited. It means simply a lesser member of a sun-system or family; generally a body which has once been extremely hot and has now lost a large degree of its heat, although in some instances it may still give forth a good deal, and may even shine to some extent.

We call a house "a house," whether it is full of people or quite empty, whether it is in good repair or unfit for use. And we call a cooled heavenly body, belonging to some central sun, a "world," whether or not living creatures could or do find a home on it.

Any single planet in the sky, whether among the many worlds of our Solar System or whether in other parts of the Universe and much too far away for their soft shining or their reflected light to be able to reach our eyes, *may* have been formed for the express purpose of sooner or later supporting life. It may be an inhabited sphere now. It *may* have been inhabited long ago, in ages past. It *may* be going to be inhabited by and by, in centuries or millenniums still distant. In such cases, we cannot get beyond a "may-be."

The very existence of such worlds, lying far beyond the limits of our Solar System, can only be a matter of conjecture, though with many minds, the conjecture means very strong probability.

But as to the question of life in them, any such life as we know here — and even of life in the worlds which we do know to exist, because we see them in our sky — we still have only conjecture to help us.

True, we may form some idea as to which of our neighbor-planets seems to be more likely than others to have reached a stage which is possibly fitted for some kind of living inhabitants. Yet the said idea has to be built largely on a foundation of "perhapses."

II. - THE PATHWAY OF VENUS

Of all the planets in our system, Venus comes first in brightness and beauty. Not only is she, from our point of view, the fairest, and the most easily found and followed, but also she is the one — with the exception only of a tiny minor planet — which at intervals draws most closely to Earth. In some ways, she may be looked upon as Earth's twin-sister.

Though in the following lines Wordsworth does not speak of her actually by name, his meaning is evident -

> "Why repine,
> Now when the Star of Eve comes forth to shine
> On British waters with that look benign?
> Ye mariners that plough your onward way,
> Or in the haven rest, or sheltering bay,
> May silent thanks at least to God be given
> With a full heart — our thoughts are heard in Heaven."

And again, we have from Longfellow:

> "Lo, in the painted oriel of the West,
>   Whose panes the sunken sun incarnadines
>   Like a fair lady at her casement shines,
> The Evening Star, the star of love and rest."

But Venus, as explained before, is no star. She is a cooled and dark body. When the Sun shines on any part of her surface, that part shines

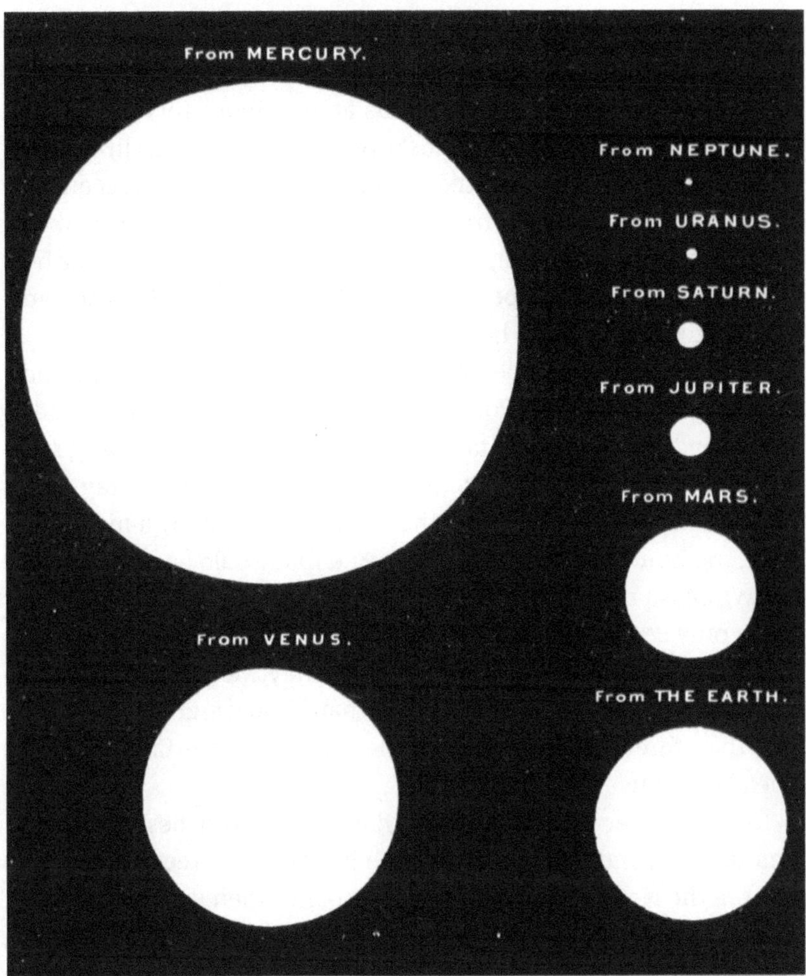

COMPARATIVE APPARENT SIZES OF THE SUN AS SEEN FROM THE VARIOUS PLANETS

in response; when any part is turned away from him, that part is in darkness. In size, she matches our Earth, being slightly smaller. The diameter of Earth is 7,927 miles, that of Venus is 7,701 miles.

Both journey round the Sun, each in its own pathway; that of Venus lying inside that of Earth, while that of Mars is outside that of Earth.

Mercury's orbit is, roughly, about half as far from the Sun as the orbit of Venus; and the orbit of Venus is about two-thirds as far as that of Earth. Counted in millions of miles, the three distances may be given as: thirty-six, sixty-seven, and ninety-three million miles.

This means, of course, for Venus an enormous increase of heat and of light, far beyond the utmost ever known here, even in our most blazing tropic regions. And the seeming size of the Sun as seen from there must be fully one-third larger than as seen from here, and very much more dazzling. Compared with Mercury's experiences, the heat and glare might perhaps be reckoned as fairly moderate; but compared with aught that we have here, they must be overwhelming.

Though we speak truly of that fair world as the "nearest to ourselves," such nearness is only occasional. She has a shorter road to travel, and she goes much faster than we do. This is necessary, since her greater nearness to the Sun means a more powerful drag on his part; and unless she balanced the added attraction by a more rapid rush, she would fall down upon him. And that would be an end of her!

While we take twelve months to get once round the Sun, Venus takes only seven and a half of our months, and she often overtakes and passes the slower Earth. In the same way, Mercury, whose pathway lies closer still, goes much faster than Venus; and his "year" lasts less than three of our months. So he constantly overtakes and runs ahead of Venus.

When at her nearest point to Earth, the latter lies between us and the Sun, and then we do not see her at all — precisely as we do not see the New Moon, because she, too, lies then just between. But when Venus has passed round to one side, we begin — in a telescope, though not with the naked eye — to make out a small crescent-shape which gradually widens to half-Venus, like the crescent-Moon and half-Moon. The latter is our very best view of the planet. Later, she travels on beyond the Sun; and though after sunset or before sunrise, we may then get a sight of her full face, the greater distance renders her a much less radiant object than when seen at the halfway positions.

These "phases" of Venus were first seen by Galileo, the famous Italian astronomer of the seventeenth century, through his telescope, one of the earliest made. But a hundred years sooner, Copernicus had foretold that, if the then new and "modern" astronomy were correct, both Mercury and Venus ought to have phases like the Moon. His foretelling proved to be true.

Mercury's phases are not so easily made out as those of Venus, because that planet is smaller, and also farther from us, and is so often lost in the Sun's shining. But both are in much the same position with regard to Earth and Sun as is our Moon. All three shine by reflected light only; all three are at times between Earth and Sun; and with all three, we can in general see that part alone which is lighted up by sunshine, and which happens also to be turned in our direction.

III. - POSSIBLE CLIMATES

You may have noticed more than once that something is mentioned as *generally seen*; and that implies, of course, that exceptions exist.

One such exception was given earlier. Now and again, when the shining crescent-Moon appears, a round dim body can be detected in that crescent. The dark side, turned away from the Sun, and usually invisible, gains a dim illumination from the Earth's brightness, and so becomes visible.

Sometimes, though not often, the same has been noticed with Venus. A small, dim body was seen "in the arms" of the little crescent-Venus. This is curious, for it cannot be due to the same cause, since the Earth is too far off to give sufficient light. It has been supposed to be brought about by a kind of "twilight-effect" — very deep atmosphere conveying the sunlight.

On another occasion, which recurs regularly, both Venus and Mercury are seen as dark bodies, their bright faces being turned completely away from us. It happens when the one or the other passes exactly between Earth and Sun; not any higher, not any lower; so that the tiny black spot may be watched through a telescope, traveling across the radiant disc.

These "Transits of Venus" take place only twice in the course of one hundred and eight years, and they used to be eagerly awaited, as a means of measuring the Sun's distance.

A perplexing question, which still remains unsettled, is the length of time taken by Venus to spin on her axis. In other words, what is the length of her "day"?

Earth spins incessantly, like a gigantic top, once in twenty-four hours. Other planets spin in like manner, some faster, some more slowly. Also, the Moon spins; the Sun spins; all other moons in our system spin; and no doubt every star in the universe goes through its own rotation at its own particular speed.

But the whirl of our fair neighbor has not been easy to make out. She is always enwrapped in such dense masses of cloud that no surface markings of the planet itself can be watched. Spots on the Sun can be followed, and markings on Mars are more or less permanent; but Venus gives no help to astronomers.

Certain hazy spots or shadows are indeed visible at times on the outer cloudy surface, and from their sluggish advance, it was thought that Venus' spin must be a very slow one. Other observers refuse to accept this, counting that cloud movements and changes are too uncertain to be depended on.

So, while some astronomers are inclined to hold that Venus has a "day" much the same in length as our own, others lean to the belief that she rotates on her axis in the same time exactly that she journeys round the Sun. If this be the case, her day and her year are one. Also, as the Moon, revolving round the Earth, turns always one side towards us, so Venus, revolving round the Sun, would turn always one side towards him.

Such a state of things would greatly affect the climate of our twin-world. Part of her surface would know no night; another part would know no day. Part would have perpetual summer; and part would live in unbroken winter. Over part would shine a blazing, dazzling Sun, fixed changelessly in her sky; over another part would brood unalterable night; and between the two would lie zones of ceaseless twilight.

Some modifications are, indeed, possible. The very density of the atmosphere, while veiling the glare on one side, might carry round some degree of twilight to a large portion of the dark side, if not to the whole of it.

Even if the atmosphere does thus modify matters, or even if the "day" is really no longer than our own, still the climate would leave a good deal to be desired. It may be that a man, living on the solid ground beneath that white envelope, could never gain a glimpse of either the Sun or stars. This does not give an impression of a very cheerful world.

The radiance of that envelope, as seen from outside, is extraordinary. Its brightness, compared with the light of Mercury, has been compared with the brightness of polished silver in full sunshine, side by side with that of lead or zinc.

One might imagine that a planet so formed, and so veiled by clouds, would need a Moon; yet Venus has no satellite.

PART VI

A RED PLANET

I. - WHAT WE SEE OF MARS

RED, but not altogether red. When that little world is seen through a telescope, yellows and greys and greens are visible also; brilliant greens sometimes. But the prevailing tint seems to be red.

Mars is by no means one of the brightest planets in our sky. He is not nearly so bright as Venus, our next-door neighbor on the other side, nor as Jupiter, our biggest brother-world. Quite a small globe, in fact larger than Mercury, and much larger than the Moon, yet utterly insignificant beside Jupiter or Saturn; and a great deal farther from the Sun than Venus or the Earth. Such is Mars.

Yet not one other world in the system of the Sun, unless we except the Moon, can be so closely studied. We know far more about the surface of this small, reddish planet than we do about Mercury or Venus, Jupiter or Saturn; even though Venus does come closer to us, and though Jupiter is so huge in size.

When, as sometimes happens, Venus, Earth, and Mars are all three at the same time on one side of the Sun, and all three are at their very nearest each to the Sun and each to the others, then Venus and Earth are about twenty-three million miles apart, and Earth and Mars are about thirty-five million miles apart.

Rather a big leap from the distance of the Moon! Tens of millions of miles instead of only between two and three hundred thousand miles.

A telescope, of course, brings Mars practically nearer, just as it brings the Moon practically nearer. How much nearer it is not easy to say with exactitude. A great deal depends, not only on the size and power of a telescope, but also on what is called "clear definition" — that is, on sharpness of outline, largely dependent on the state of the atmosphere, on the absence of haze, and on other matters. A telescope of lesser powers will often give better results than a very big one.

With the Moon, we found that objects could be fairly well seen which were not in size more than two or three miles across, such as a small crater, three miles in diameter.

With Mars, not nearly so much can be expected. Think what thirty-five million miles really means, and how much, or how little, can be seen on Earth even one or two hundred miles away.

It is not often that the three worlds are in just that position — in a direct line one with another and with the Sun. When they are, Venus lies between us and the Sun, with her bright side turned away, so that we cannot see her at all, till she gets round a little to one side. But Mars, being outside our orbit, turns his full and illumined face right towards us; and we have then a really good view.

Really good — considering the distance!

Looking at him thus, through even the most powerful telescopes and under the best conditions, does not mean what people at one time seemed to think it ought. It does not mean seeing human beings, or trees, or villages, or towns. But it does mean seeing more than can be seen on any other planet in our system, or in the whole universe.

It means seeing hazy outlines, which probably may be lands, continents, ocean beds; and ice caps hundreds of miles in diameter; and clouds or masses of cloud; and mysterious straight lines, also hundreds of miles in length; and faint signs here and there of possible vegetation.

With Venus, so far as we can tell, we seldom if ever catch a glimpse of the actual body of the planet, but only look on her dazzling vesture of clouds. With Mars, things are widely different. Not only do we constantly look on his solid surface, but we can study its changes, note its varieties of seasons, measure the extent of its snow caps in different months, and of its — probable — lakes and streams, and even speculate on the growth of its — possible — vegetation.

MARS

For the surface of this celestial friend of ours shows a variety of markings of one kind and another; some of which observers are more and more sure must mean certain realities.

That astronomers are not fully agreed on such subjects need not worry or discourage anybody. Like all human beings, observers of heavenly bodies are liable to make mistakes, and even to be for a time quite convinced of explanations which later are proved to be wrong. Half the scientific knowledge which we now possess is built upon the ruins of past errors; and many of the theories which are widely accepted at this moment may have in time to give place to other and more remarkable realities.

And even when the theories or explanations offered are not right, and must in time be displaced by others, still it has been better to know all along that some sort of understanding of the puzzle was within our reach, than to have been utterly and hopelessly nonplussed.

This was once pointed out to me by a wise and able clergyman friend, with regard to certain deeper mysteries on questions yet more profound. "What I say may not be the right explanation," he said. "But it is good to know that *some* explanation is possible, though the real one may be different and far more wonderful."

His words, true of the mightier mysteries of life and death, are true also about these lesser perplexities. It is worthwhile to conjecture a way out — worth while to find some sort of possible clue — even though our conjectures may someday prove to be mistaken.

Only, it is also well to avoid over-positiveness, and to be willing to find ourselves in the wrong. Which means willingness to accept readily fresh light thrown upon difficult questions when it comes.

II. - TWO LITTLE MOONS

Mars, in place of being nearly eight thousand miles through like Earth and Venus, is only about four thousand three hundred miles, and his weight is about one-ninth that of Earth. This means a greatly lessened power of attraction for things on his surface.

It means, too, that objects on that world weigh much less than they would weigh on Earth; the downward drag being so much slighter. A strong man here can at most leap only a few feet into the air. But on Mars, the effort which here carries him up three or four feet might there lift him easily over a good-sized house — if houses are built on Mars. All our systems of weights and measures would have to be altered for use under such conditions.

Still, thus far that little world has been able to keep possession of an atmosphere, or at all events of a good deal of it, instead of losing practically the whole, like the Moon.

Two tiny moons travel with the Red World in his annual journey round the Sun, on an orbit about half as far off again as the orbit of Earth. Their names are Phobos and Deimos, and the bigger of the two is a mere large ball, some twenty miles in diameter. Which is to say that it could be placed between two of our towns, lying twenty-five miles apart, without touching either. Not, however, without overshadowing either, for it would tower twenty miles high in the air.

Phobos journeys at a fine rate round Mars — his "primary," as a planet is always called with reference to any of his moons — getting round once in about seven hours and a half, instead of taking four weeks for the tour, as our Moon does. So, if Mars, or Mars' inhabitants, should reckon the months by the biggest and nearest moon, the result would be three Martian months in one Martian day! A very curious arrangement according to our earthly notions. The "day" of Mars, due to his spin on his axis, lasts slightly longer than our earthly day.

But the *year* of Mars is not far short of two earthly years. Not only is his pathway longer than ours, just as ours is longer than the orbit of Venus, but also his pace is slower than ours, precisely as ours is slower than that of Venus, and for the same reason. Because the distance is greater, the drawing power of the Sun is less; and because that drawing power is less, Mars does not need to travel so fast as Earth to avoid being dragged down upon the Sun. Each planet's speed has to be exactly enough to counterbalance the Sun's pull.

A remarkable sight on the planet is its apparent snow-caps, real white caps, at the north and south poles. In studying other worlds of our Solar System, we naturally give them earthly names; and not only to the worlds as a whole, but to parts of those worlds. We speak of the north pole, the south pole, the equator, and so on, of each; and the position of poles and equator is settled by the slant of the planet's axis. Sometimes that *slant* is greater, sometimes it is less than the slant of Earth's axis. This slant is always with reference to the plane of the ecliptic.

Of course, you know already that the ecliptic is the seeming path of the Sun through the year, among certain constellations; the line along which he appears to travel, in consequence of our own annual journey round him, which causes us to see him against one group of stars after another.

And the plane of the ecliptic is the flat surface — if such a term may be used where there is no surface — which lies within the whole circle of that ecliptic. You may draw a circle on a piece of paper, and the plane of that circle is the part of the paper which it encloses; only the paper must lie flat, or it would not be a plane. Or, again, you may imagine a circle in the air, formed by a slender wreath of smoke, and the *plane* of that circle would be the round space enclosed by the smoke; only, once more, it must be level in shape, or it could not be called a plane.

All the planets of our system keep very nearly — not *quite*, but *nearly* — to the plane or the level of the ecliptic; and all, or nearly all, the planets' axes slant a little to that plane. They do not stand bolt upright to it, but lie slightly over.

It is this slant of the axis of our Earth which gives us the various seasons; and if our axis were bolt upright, we should have the same weather all the year round, over all the Earth. With other planets, their weather is greatly affected by the degree in which the axis of each stands more upright or leans more over towards the plane of the ecliptic.

Mars, like the rest, has a slant. This means that his two poles — like our two poles — take turns in the course of the planet's year to be turned towards the Sun and away from the Sun. And *this* means, as with us, the summers and winters of the northern and southern hemispheres. So Mars, like Earth, has summers and winters and intervening half-seasons.

In one part of his long year, when the northern hemisphere is towards the Sun, the northern half has summer and the southern half has winter. Then, when he has traveled round to the opposite side of the Sun, turning towards him the south pole, summer reigns over the southern half and winter grips the northern half.

And the two poles of Mars are clothed, each one, with a white cap. Snow and ice, of course! Well, not quite "of course." Through many years, doubts were freely expressed, and other possible substances, in place of water, such as carbonic acid, were discussed. Now, however, it seems pretty generally accepted as fairly certain that those white caps really and truly are ice and snow, like our own northern and southern ice caps!

During the summer of each pole in turn, when that pole is turned towards the Sun, its ice cap grows visibly smaller; and during the winter of each pole, when that pole is turned away from the Sun, its ice cap grows visibly larger. These changes have been again and again noted, and the varying sizes of the ice caps have been measured.

Thawing is sometimes seen to take place very quickly. In only six days, the boundary-line of one cap shrank to an extent of six hundred miles. So great a mass of snow would result in a huge volume of water.

Clouds seem to be fairly common; not vast masses like those which clothe Venus, but extensive enough to be seen from Earth. They change and grow and melt away, much as our clouds do.

And if there is an atmosphere, and if there are clouds and snow, we may be sure that there is also rain, perhaps in parts very heavy rain. Which makes it probable that floods take place at times. And this, again, would mean the movement of big supplies of water from one place to another.

Among the varied tints and dim outlines seen on Mars, parts were long looked upon as "land" and "water." This in time was given up, and the notion of any kind of "oceans" was scouted. But another modification has crept in, and while it is still held that no large *permanent* oceans are found, yet bodies of water do exist. The melting of hundreds of square miles of snow, even though the snow may not be very deep, would ensure such a result.

Such "seas," as they are often called, are sometimes seen to grow at a startling rate. In one place, on a certain day, no signs of water were visible. But within three days, a considerable lake had made its appearance there, hundreds of miles long and broad. Judging from its bright surface and its blue color, little doubt could be felt that it really was water.

> "There is no light in earth or heaven
> But the cold light of stars,
> And the first watch of night is given
> To the red planet, Mars.
>
> Is it the tender star of love?
> The star of love and dreams?
> O no, from that blue tent above
> A hero's armor gleams.

And earnest thoughts within me rise
　　When I behold afar,
Suspended in the evening skies,
　　The shield of that red star.

O star of strength, I see thee stand
　　And smile upon my pain;
Thou beckonest with that mailed hand,
　　And I am strong again.

Within my breast there is no light,
　　But the cold light of stars;
I give the first watch of the night
　　To the red planet, Mars."[8]

LONGFELLOW

---

[8]　　This ruddy world - which, despite all poetic assertions, is no star - was named after "the god of war," the Mars of ancient mythology.

III. - CANALS AND MARSHES

Some curious straight lines have been seen from time to time on Mars, claiming attention. It was long questioned whether they meant anything real — whether they might not be due to imagination. But there the lines are, unmistakably; and they certainly mean something.

A rather unfortunate name was given to them at first, and it has clung ever since, as the most meaningless names have a trick of doing. They were called CANALS.

Our earthly conception of a canal is an artificial watercourse made by man. Naturally, people in general at once supposed that canals on Mars must be the same in kind, made by beings such as ourselves. Certain astronomers have warmly upheld the idea, while others have refused to accept it as even probable.

We sometimes speak of "Martians," as if we knew that they really existed. Of course, we do not know. They may be there. No human being can declare that it is impossible. But we have no reliable proofs whatever that it is so, though certain indications may seem to point to the possibility. At the best, we can only suppose, and imagine, and conjecture.

At first, only two or three lines were seen; but as time went on, and observations also went on, many more were detected, till at length a real network of them could be drawn over the face of the planet, looking not unlike a spider's web. Some astronomers see them very clearly. Others have frankly confessed their inability to make them out at all.

The first point which struck everybody was their extraordinary straightness; and this it was, no doubt, which first suggested the notion of "canals." Still, it must be remembered that "straightness in objects tens of millions of miles distant does not, or need not, mean the same as "straightness" in an object near at hand. A river, seen on Earth from a distance of one or two hundred miles, would probably look straight; yet, when viewed from near at hand, it would have any number of bends and curves.

These "canals" were at first regarded as almost certainly — whether natural or artificial — intended for the carrying away of melted snows from the north pole southward; and perhaps also for the support of vegetation.

Then doubts arose. It was found that a canal would sometimes run right through a part which had been looked upon as a probable sea. This, if the sea were really a sea, would pretty well prove that the canal was not a canal. Or, if the canal were really a canal, it would prove that the sea was not a sea. Again, it appeared that the so-called "canals" were not always fixed in certain places, but that some of them seemed to change their positions, to shift about, to disappear and reappear, perhaps following fresh courses.

All these things were puzzling. Moreover, the canals were found to be much bigger than was first imagined — much longer, much broader. It became difficult to think that any beings like ourselves could have constructed them.

It is still held that they may be channels, which serve to carry off masses of water from the polar regions, perhaps depositing that water in large lakes or beds. But another difficulty comes in here. If Mars is so very flat a world as it seems to be, there can be little of uphill and downhill; and how, then, could water in large quantities flow constantly from one part to another? The idea reminds one of a phrase used by Robert Montgomery in one of his poems, and mercilessly criticised by Macaulay -

> "The soul aspiring, pants its source to mount,
> As streams meander level with their fount."

No stream meanders, or can possibly meander, level with its fount," declared the indignant Essayist. If so, how do the streams find their way in Mars?

A new suggestion has been more lately made. What if, in place of being something in the nature of canals or rivers, these long lines are really somewhat extensive *marshes*; not so much carrying onward but rather holding back the supplies of water from snows and rains? Perhaps the real danger is of such water disappearing too quickly into the atmosphere, or spreading about too quickly in thin layers, easily dissipated. Without some sort of natural — or, if you like, artificial — "reservoirs," this might take place. If such be the work of those "canals," they would be doing for Mars, to some extent, the work which our oceans do for us on Earth.

Probably only the larger and more permanent canals should be thus described — as broad marshlands, supporting plant life of various kinds along their length. Whether the smaller and less stable canals are to any degree the same — whether, also, these might indeed have been constructed by Martian inhabitants to carry on the same work in regions devoid of greater marshlands — whether, therefore, they may support not only vegetable life, but also animal life, and possibly the life of beings not totally unlike ourselves—these are questions which may at least be discussed, though at present no decisive replies can be given.

Such great marshes, perhaps from fifteen to twenty miles wide, in parts widening to what are termed "oases," averaging a hundred and twenty miles across, might be fed at times by heavy rains, as well as by the melting of winter snows near the poles. The changes of tints, seen with varying seasons on some of the larger canals, are believed to tell of these developments. Greenish hues may mean the growth of vegetation; bluish hues may mean fresh floodings of water.

But such conjectures, while most interesting, should be received with caution in the present state of our knowledge.

A good deal has been written about the "doubling" of the canals, two being seen close, side by side, where only one had been. "Close," that is, as viewed from tens of millions of miles away. This doubling has been sometimes used as an additional argument in proof of the canals having been — perhaps — made by reasoning beings.

It is rather remarkable that of late similar "canals" have been seen on our much nearer neighbour, the Moon. Some astronomers indeed disbelieve in their existence, and they have been alluded to as "spurious canals;" while others maintain that they are most distinctly visible. One "double-canal" is described as running straight onward, the two halves side by side, for mile after mile, climbing a height of four thousand feet and descending on the other side. And the most singular part of the matter is that these lunar canals—so it is stated—have precisely the same "artificial appearance" as the Martian canals; giving strongly the impression that they might have been made by intelligent beings for purposes of conveying water to where it was needed.

In a world which is practically without air, and probably without at least running water, it is difficult to imagine that such canals for such a purpose could, under present conditions, be required, and it is impossible to believe that any beings at all, with life such as that of man, could exist.

One astronomer[9] has distinctly asserted that "any conclusion derived from the Martian canals should apply to those of the Moon, and *vice versa*." This view might perhaps rather tend to shake our belief that such artificial water-courses exist in Mars than to persuade us that they are both needed and supplied in the Moon.

A few more words on this much-debated question. The possibility has been several times alluded to in past pages. But it is a question on which we find ourselves in the dark.

Not even the almost certainty of an atmosphere, with mists and clouds, rain and snow, wind and sunshine, and probable water-courses or marshes, can settle it. Mars seems to possess all these; yet that little world may not be fitted for living creatures, such as are known to us.

True, there is an atmosphere; but one very unlike ours. The small size of that globe causes a great difference. For the powerful attraction which on Earth binds the air to the ground, and packs it in dense

9   Professor W. H. Pickering

layers for us to breathe, is lacking with Mars. Gravitation there must be extremely weak by comparison; and the atmosphere, even close down on the ground, cannot but be excessively thin.

Mountain climbers on Earth find the rarefied air at great heights difficult to breathe; and the air of Mars must be far more thin than on our highest mountains. This would be balanced, to some extent, by the lessened weight of living creatures. And there is also a great deal in what we are used to. Those who at first can hardly breathe on some great height, may yet learn to live there. In time they cease to suffer, as their hearts and lungs adapt themselves to the new conditions.

So we may not say that some such creatures as are found on Earth could not possibly live in Mars' atmosphere. We can only say that these and other facts add to the difficulties of the question.

A favourite argument, often put forward, is that of the planets' use. Those bright worlds in the sky, we are told, cannot have been made for no purpose. He who "formed not our Earth in vain, but made it to be inhabited,"[10] *must* have done the same with other worlds.

It is always rash to use a "must-be" argument in matters where we really are in ignorance. That it may be so, we can safely say; and that, so far as the general argument goes, it does not seem unreasonable.

The Eternal Father, we may be sure, does not create in vain, though to our short sight it may sometimes seem as if He did.

What of the enormous wealth of apparently wasted sunbeams? What of the myriad flowers which bloom and die unseen — unseen, at least, by man? There is the point. Man is not the only being who deserves consideration; and his share in the Universe is not, as yet, very great.

Whether a flower is enjoyed by men, whether worlds and suns are made for objects which men can understand — that often is the true meaning of our questionings. But God sees the little flower blooming in the wilderness; and God has uses for these bright worlds, perhaps unlike and beyond any possibilities which we can grasp. The Universe, after all, was not planned on nineteenth- and twentieth-century business notions.

10   Isa. xlv. 18.

We may freely grant that each fair world was created with some object, and that the said object is sometimes one which we can grasp; such as, to be the home of living creatures. Our Earth was so made and prepared, and other worlds may have been put together with a like intention; some at least of them, not necessarily all.

But another fact comes in. Our Earth went through a long and slow making-ready for this purpose. Ages rolled by, and still the Earth was uninhabited by even the lower forms of life. Ages more passed, after their appearance, before the higher forms followed.

If this was so with our world, why not with other worlds too?

The smaller a planet may be in size, the more rapidly it may ripen for use. First comes the stage of cooling; if, as we believe, they all were at one time greatly heated; and a lengthy stage this is. But a smaller body gets through its cooling faster than a large body.

It has been reckoned that Mars may have grown cool more than two and a half times as fast as our Earth, and the following calcula-tion has been made.

Suppose it happened that Earth and Mars started their cooling together — for the sake of argument, about eighteen million years ago was suggested as an imaginary date — and suppose that they kept up their cooling at about the same steady pace; then Mars would have reached a state answering to the Earth's present condition about *eleven million years ago*.

And during those eleven million years, Mars might have cooled further as much as our Earth might be expected to cool in the course of *another twenty-eight million years*. For the Earth, though cool enough for us to live on her outer surface, is by no means thoroughly cool all through, but is believed to be exceedingly hot still, deep down inside.

All this complicates still more the difficult question of life or non-life on Mars.

It *may* be that the living history of Mars lies in the far past, that it is over now, and that the little planet, like some used-up hulk, tossed aside, floats on the wide expanse of Space, no longer the abode of living beings.

Yet, even if it were so — and we have no proof whatever that it is — who should venture to say that no further use for Mars can exist in the ages to come? The very materials of some old, used-up hulk may be re-fashioned into new shapes for use and for beauty. There are not only mysteries but also possibilities in the story of the Universe, beyond our ken.

PART VII

GIANT WORLDS

I. - LITTLE AND GREAT

BETWEEN Mars and the next important member of the Sun's family lies a wide space, occupied by a number of very small bodies, commonly now spoken of as THE MINOR PLANETS. In the past, they were known as the "Asteroids" or Little Stars, then as the "Planetoids" or Little Planets, which last they are — but *not* stars.

The biggest of these, Ceres, is only about four hundred and eighty miles in diameter — a mere pigmy beside our Moon. From thence, they range downward to what are simply large balls rolling through the sky. At first, their numbers were supposed to be few — perhaps twenty or thirty at most. But more and more were gradually sighted, named, and charted, until now at least close upon a thousand are known to astronomers. How many hundreds or thousands more may remain to be discovered, time alone can show.

For a good while, they were believed to keep strictly to a certain limited district or belt, in the regions which divide the orbit of Mars from the orbit of Jupiter, behaving in a most orderly and obedient fashion — obedient, I mean, to our ideas of what they might be expected to do.

But in recent years, some wandering members of that company have been found outside the said limits.

One of these, Eros, by name, is especially interesting — not on account of its size, for it is a mere ball, perhaps only twenty miles through, or about the size of Mars' moon, Phobos, but on account of its position. Instead of keeping to the wide belt, which is followed by most

of its companions, this ambitious planetoid, during part of its year —
for even minor planets have their own separate "years" — travels right
away between Mars and Earth. It actually has the self-assertion to draw
much closer to us than any other heavenly body in the sky, except our
Moon—nearer than our next-door neighbors, Mars and Venus.

Another minute minor, no less adventurous, and so unimportant in
itself that it can boast no name but is distinguished simply as T.G. 588,
instead of coming farther this way, goes farther off than anyone would

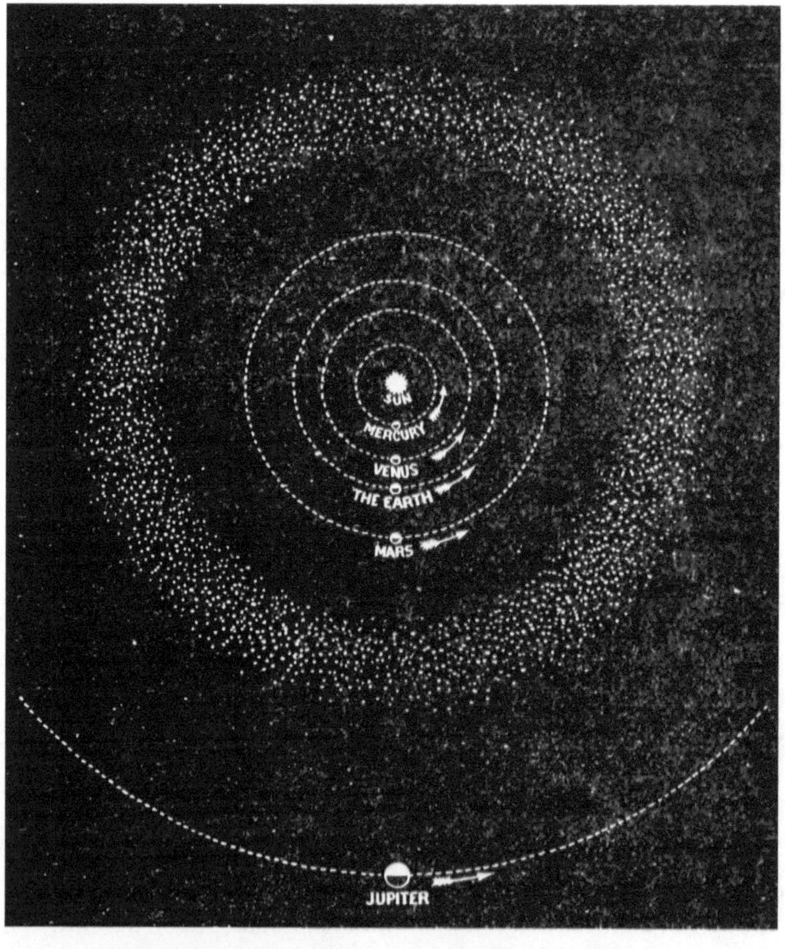

THE MINOR PLANETS BETWEEN MARS AND JUPITER

expect. During part of its "year," it has the presumption to approach very nearly, if it does not actually cross, Jupiter's pathway.

The contrast between this tiny ball and the vast bulk of Jupiter makes one irresistibly think of Landseer's famous picture, "Dignity and Impudence."

It was long held that the minor planets might be scattered remnants of a single large world, which had somehow broken up or gone to pieces in ages past, scattering its pieces far and wide. This is not now generally looked upon as so likely. They are regarded rather as genuine small planets, each having its own individual pathway around the Sun, though each is perpetually swayed and influenced by the drawing power of bigger heavenly bodies passing near.

Leaving Mars behind us, with only this brief glance by the way at the hundreds of little hurrying bodies between, we journey on to the giant-world of our System, JUPITER. And that giant-world lies nearly five times as far off from the central Sun as our Earth does. Think of that — *five times ninety-three million miles*! Not easy to picture in one's mind.

Other worlds lie farther still. Jupiter's twin-giant, SATURN, has the next nearest position. But Saturn's orbit is about twice as far from the Sun as Jupiter's orbit, which it encircles. The third great outer planet, URANUS, follows its lonely path, twice as far from the Sun as that of Jupiter; and the fourth, NEPTUNE, lags along his dim and dreary way, as far from Uranus as Uranus is from Saturn.

Huge planets, all of these, though the two last-named are not nearly so huge as the two first. All four shine, like the lesser worlds, with the borrowed radiance of sunlight, though it is thought probable that they also give forth some shining of their own.

But not one among them all is so brilliant an orb, seen from Earth, as Jupiter. Venus alone in our sky can outshine him.

Like Venus and Mars, he does not beam upon us at all times with equal brightness, for sometimes he is nearer, being on the same side of the Sun as we are; sometimes he is more distant, being on the opposite side. And even when he and we are on one side, the dividing distance varies much, because of the extremely oval — or elliptic — shape of Jupiter's pathway. It is only about once in twelve years that the two

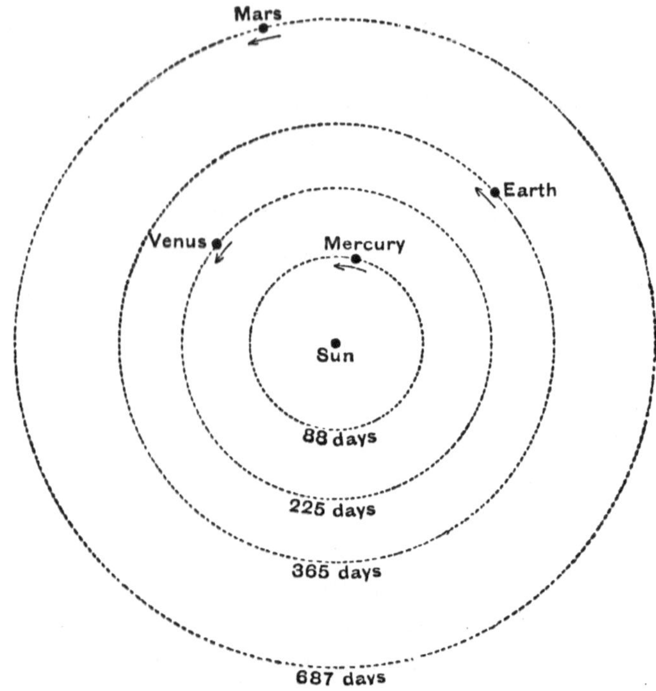

DIFFERING LENGTHS OF THE PLANET-YEARS, MERCURY TO MARS

planets reach their very nearest points, so that we see our big brother-world at his very best. Then he is indeed beautiful.

Jupiter is by far the biggest world in our System, though Saturn comes near enough to be called his "twin." Our Earth and her twin, Venus, are each nearly eight thousand miles in diameter. But the diameter of Jupiter is about eighty-five thousand miles. Quite enormous compared with the globe on which we live, but not at all enormous compared with the Sun.

About eleven Earths might be strung on a massive wire and placed within Jupiter, reaching from one side to the other, at his equator. But about the same number of Jupiters might be strung on a yet more massive wire and placed within the body of the Sun, reaching to either side. Also, something like one thousand Earths might be packed inside a hollow globe the size of Jupiter. But something like one thousand Jupiters might be packed inside a greater hollow globe, the size of the Sun.

In shape, this planet is much flattened at the poles and much bulged

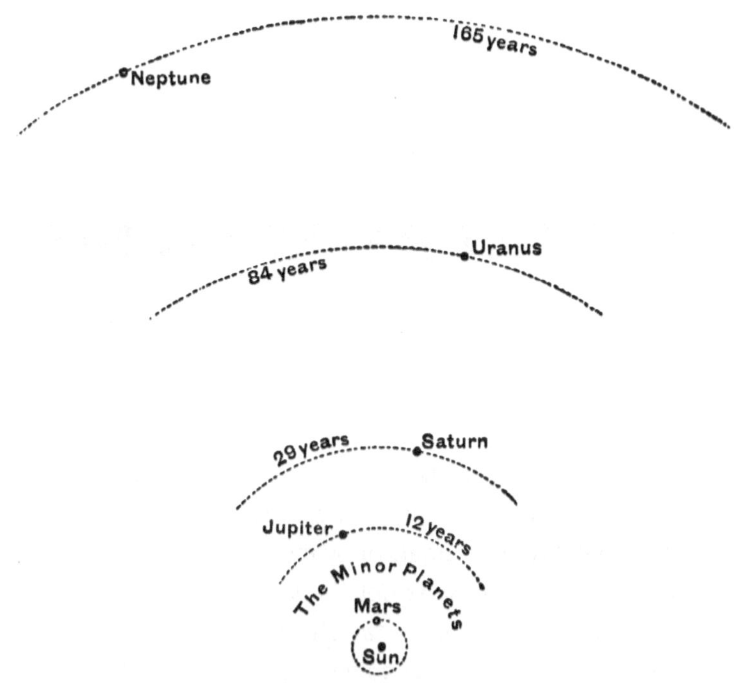

DIFFERING LENGTHS OF THE PLANET-YEARS, JUPITER TO NEPTUNE

out at the equator, and he spins on his axis at a fine rate, whirling completely round in less than ten earthly hours, which means that he has a day of only five hours and a night of the same, inclusive of twilight. His axis is placed very nearly upright to the "Plane of the Ecliptic," instead of sloping like that of Earth. This would mean little or no season-changes. If he had seasons, such as ours, they would be very lengthy, since a single "year" on Jupiter lasts through nearly twelve of our years.

Yet this long year of his is short compared with others. For Saturn's "year" lasts through nearly thirty of ours; and Uranus' "year" through eighty-four of ours; and Neptune's "year" through one hundred and sixty-five of ours.

II. - STILL RATHER WARM

Though it is right to speak of Jupiter, in a sense, as a "world," this must not be taken to mean a planet which is inhabited, or even which is fit to be inhabited by animals or by men.

Jupiter is not a Sun. He is not the scene of fiercely-heated and intensely-glowing gases like a star. Nevertheless, he cannot be said to have reached the calm and cooled condition of our Earth.

We saw how it may be that Mars long ago passed through the particular stage of existence in which Earth now is. But without any "may be," we can confidently say that Jupiter is far from having come anywhere near the present state of our little world, being rather in the condition which we suppose to have been ours long ages ago.

You have heard how a large, heated globe must always take longer to cool than a small heated globe of the same materials. This is not difficult to prove. If you had three iron balls — one the size of a marble, one the size of an orange, one the size of a school-globe — if you could heat them all to red-heat in a furnace and could then set them aside to cool, you would see for yourself. The small one would grow cold first; then the medium-sized one; and lastly the big one.

And in the slow cooling of stars and worlds, the same is found.

Mars, being a very small globe, must have cooled far more quickly than our Earth, though not so fast as Mercury, which is smaller still. Venus is in bulk much the same as Earth, and if we could penetrate her veil of clouds, we might find her to be at somewhere about the same stage as ourselves.

With Jupiter and the other three outer planets, matters are widely different.

So far as size is concerned, Jupiter is equal to some thirteen hundred Earths. But he is so much lighter in make that, so far as weight is concerned, he is equal only to about three hundred and twenty Earths.

And the explanation is not hard to find. A body weighs more or less according to its make — according to the number of tiny particles which are packed into a given space. A solid mass is heavier than a liquid mass, and a liquid mass is heavier than a vaporous or gaseous mass; because the particles lie more closely together in a solid than in a liquid, and more closely together in a liquid than in a gas or vapour.

Our Earth, being on the whole cool and solid, weighs more than another body of the same size but of a looser make. And whatever the inside condition of Jupiter may be, the vast outer cloudy covering is not solid, is not even in the main liquid. As that huge body grows more cool, it will shrink into a smaller size; and since the materials will then be more closely pressed together, it will weigh more in proportion to its bulk.

But though so light in form, weighing hardly, if at all, more than an equal body of water, the planet's enormous size gives him a force of attraction far beyond what we know here.

If you and I could be somehow transported thither, and could stand on his surface — though to talk of standing upon masses of heated cloud and scalding steam has a curious sound! — we should find ourselves to be amazingly heavier than on Earth. In fact, it would be no question of *standing*, for we should be dragged downward with such force as to be compelled to lie flat, helpless and overpowered — if, again, one could be supposed to lie down on such a surface and not instantly sink through to the uttermost depths.

A child, weighing here only six stone, would there weigh about fifteen stone. A man, weighing here twelve stone, would there weigh something like thirty stone. Human muscles could not manage so unwieldy a body.

Jupiter's markings are far more beautiful than any on Venus or Mars. Lovely belts of soft colour, red and salmon, varied by shades of blue and purple, relieved by pure white, and accentuated by dark or tinted or white spots, may be seen through a good telescope. In a general way, the broad belts are always there, though lesser changes constantly take place in them.

They are not permanent, in the sense in which certain markings on our Moon are permanent. Instead of belonging to the solid body of the planet — if such a body exists — they belong to a vast enfolding cloudland. And they are due to the terrific currents of the atmosphere, which sweep enormous masses of clouds round and round the globe, at almost unbelievable speeds.

It is because of these bands, always there though ever changing, that Jupiter has been called "The Belted Giant of our System."

His atmosphere is supposed to be at least a thousand miles in depth, and how much more, no one knows. When we realise that the entire mass of waters, which if cooled would no doubt form oceans on the surface of that globe, now appear to float aloft in a state of scalding steam or heated vapour, we may dimly picture the extent of that restless cloudland.

The most that can usually be seen, even through a large telescope and under good conditions, has been described as a "uniform white mass of cloud," over which seems spread a kind of gauzy brown veil, clothing the whole globe from north pole to south pole, but in parts more dense than elsewhere. The "belts" seem, or seemed to one observer, to be formed by denser quantities of this gauzy material.

A famous Great Red Spot was for many years under close and constant observation. Of late, it has appeared to be fading.

Jupiter's extremely rapid spin on his axis has been spoken of earlier as lasting just ten hours. Our Earth spins once in twenty-four hours; and on our equator, at this rate and in this ceaseless whirl, the ground rushes along at about one thousand miles an hour. But the surface of Jupiter, or rather of the enveloping cloud-masses over his equator, travels at a rate of more than seven miles each second. You may easily reckon how many miles an hour that will come to!

"The spacious firmament on high,
With all the blue ethereal sky
And spangled heavens, a shining frame,
Their great Original proclaim.
The unwearied Sun from day to day
Does his Creator's power display;
And publishes to every land
The work of an Almighty Hand.

"Soon as the evening shades prevail,
The Moon takes up the wondrous tale;
And nightly to the listening Earth
Repeats the story of her birth;
Whilst all the Stars that round her burn,
And all the Planets in their turn,
Confirm the tidings as they roll,
And spread the truth from pole to pole.

"What though in solemn silence all
Move round the dark terrestrial ball?
What though nor real voice nor sound
Amid their radiant orbs be found?
In Reason's ear they all rejoice,
And utter forth a glorious voice;
For ever singing, as they shine—
'The Hand that made us is Divine!'"
JOSEPH ADDISON (1792–1819)

III. - IS JUPITER INHABITED?

Not a difficult question this, to answer, if by the word is meant "inhabited by living creatures such as we know on Earth." Much easier, in fact, than when it is asked about Mars or Venus.

Though Jupiter is no longer, as he may once have been, in a state of glowing heat and intense brilliancy like the Sun, he is probably still red-hot or even white-hot. If so, no water could remain on his surface. Any finding its way thither would instantly boil and pass upward as steam, to remain floating aloft till the body of the planet should become cool enough to receive it in a liquid form.

Under such conditions, the question as to whether Jupiter may now be a world inhabited by any sort of animal or human life hardly exists. A red-hot or white-hot globe, surrounded by vast masses of scalding steam, perpetually careering about in furious cyclones, could support no life of any kind with which we are acquainted.

So if Mars *may* once have been inhabited, and *may* now have passed beyond that particular stage of usefulness, Jupiter, on the contrary, may be still undergoing a long process of preparation for — possible — future habitation.

We believe that once upon a time, long long ago, our Earth must have been a red-hot ball, with all her oceans floating overhead as heated vapour; and that she very gradually became so far cooled as to let those oceans subside on her surface as water, warm water at first, cool afterwards. Jupiter seems still to be at that early stage which we sometimes describe as "chaos."

When discussing the question of possible inhabitants for either Mars or Venus, we cannot get beyond a "maybe." But with Jupiter and the other great outer planets, we can confidently decide against any present denizens like ourselves, though what may lie in the unborn future, no man can say.

Naturally, the question may come up: If they are being made ready, how long would the course of preparation last? How soon might Jupiter be ready — supposing that he really is destined for such a purpose?

We have to remember that long ages were needed by our small world before she was in a fit state to be a home for mankind. And we must consider that, with a very much larger world, very much longer preparation would be needed, since the cooling down would be so very much slower. If Mars may be reasonably supposed to have taken millions of years *less* than our Earth, Jupiter may well be supposed to take many millions of years *more* than our Earth for that business.

And just as we found Mars to be, practically, a much older globe than Earth, and the Moon older still, so we find Jupiter to be a much younger globe than Earth; not in the number of centuries that it may have existed, but in development, in growth, in readiness for possible use. A sapling of an oak tree is much younger, practically, than a worn-out biennial plant just dying, yet the oak may have lived four times as many years as the plant.

No one can state precisely how hot Jupiter may be at the present time. But since it is held that this planet has still some power of shining, that is, of giving forth light independently of the Sun, the heat must be very great.

An iron ball might be far too greatly heated for us to touch, yet it might give forth not the faintest glimmer of light which we could see. Not till it is made red-hot should we make it out, even dimly, in darkness.

So if Jupiter does really shine with his own heat, as well as by reflection of the Sun's rays, he can hardly be less than what we describe as white-hot.

Two reasons, at least, we have for supposing that it may be so. One is that, when well placed for our observation, he is so extraordinarily bright. It could scarcely be expected, at his enormous distance from the Sun, that merely reflected shining should be so radiant. Also, when the rays arriving from Jupiter are examined with the spectroscope, those rays seem to speak, not only of reflected light, but of the planet's own independent shining.

If things are thus, though the state of Jupiter is very far from the state of a star, yet it does mean a condition of any roar of heat which seems to bang and bolt the notion of human beings living there at present.

Four attendant moons have long been known to circle round our giant brother-world, easily seen through an ordinary opera-glass; and several much smaller ones have more lately been discovered, amounting to ten in all. Others may be found as time goes on. He and his satellites make a small inner system by themselves, within the greater Solar System.

As the Moons travel round their "primary," the four principal ones keep in their orbits to much the same "plane" or level, just as the planets of the Solar System keep generally to one plane, the Plane of the Ecliptic, in their journeyings round the Sun.

At one time a suggestion was put forward that perhaps these moons might themselves be inhabited, and that Jupiter might act for them the part of a lesser sun, pouring out warmth and light to make up for the great distance of the real Sun. This idea does not, however, now find favour.

Of the four chief satellites, the two inner ones are in size much the same as our Moon, and the two outer ones are both larger than Mercury. They, like our Moon, are in reality planets travelling round and with Jupiter, and with him round the Sun. The views of Jupiter, seen from any of them, must often be magnificent, more especially from the nearer ones.

IV. - A WONDROUS PLANET

Saturn, like Jupiter, is the head of a small system of his own, within the Solar System. But his is a more marvellous family than that of Jupiter.

In size, this planet is rather the smaller of the two, and a good deal lighter in make, lighter in fact than water. If the whole big body of Saturn could be plunged into some vast ocean of water — and that ocean would have to be vast indeed for such a purpose — the globe would float as if it were an India-rubber ball.

This is a fact, known, not guessed. Strange though the idea may seem, heavenly bodies can be actually *weighed* from Earth, as if they were put into huge scales, one against another. And the mode in which it is done is by observing and calculating the *pull* of one body on another. In this manner, the actual *avoir-dupois* weight of the Moon, of planets, of the Sun, and even of certain stars, has been reckoned.

Saturn, too, has greatly flattened poles and a very bulging equator, and his big body spins rapidly round in little over ten hours. Apparently, he is covered with immense masses of clouds, though the signs of furious disturbances, ever present on Jupiter, are not so evident here. But we have to allow for the enormously increased distance, making it so much more difficult for us to see what goes on.

This large planet has been described as "a world in the making," a phrase which might equally well be used for Jupiter, and, no doubt, for Uranus and Neptune. The "making" in Saturn's case seems not to have

COMPARATIVE SIZES OF SATURN AND EARTH

advanced so far as even with Jupiter. Though smaller than his gigantic twin, he shows signs of being even less cooled, which is curious.

Not only has Saturn a family of ten moons — very likely more than ten — but also, he is surrounded by an extraordinary set of Rings, unlike anything possessed by any other member of the Sun's family.

Of the moons, the largest, Titan, is about the same size as Mercury, and takes rather more than a fortnight to journey round its big planet. But Mimas, the nearest, has to rush round in twenty-two hours, so strong is the drawing which otherwise would drag it down into that heated, cloudy surface. And while Saturn's "day" is only a little over ten earthly hours, his "year" lasts through nearly thirty of our years, as already stated.

And the Rings, those wonderful Rings which mark Saturn out as apart from all other worlds!

It is commonly said that they are three in number, one over another; that is, they are placed farther and farther away from the body of the planet. They are very wide, stretching outward from the globe, passing round the whole of it, over its equator.

To see clearly what this means, get a small globe or a large apple, and a piece of ribbon long enough to go easily once round it. Now fold the ribbon round the apple like a sash, lying flat on it. But that will not do as a picture of the Rings. You have to hold the ribbon against the apple, not lying flat, not with its *width* against the skin, but with its *edge* only touching. One edge of the ribbon must rest on the apple, and the other edge must stand outwards away from it. That is how the Rings are placed.

They are extraordinarily wide, *outward* from the planet, and extraordinarily narrow, as seen *from the surface of the planet, underneath them.*

Here are the measurements, given roughly.

To begin with, Saturn's own diameter is more than seventy-six thousand miles.

If a man stood on the equator — supposing, again, that any human being could stand there — all he would see of the Rings just overhead, if he could see anything of them at all, would be a thin line or edge, crossing the sky five or six thousand miles distant. For the Rings, like the piece of ribbon on the apple, would not lie *flat* over his head, but would be placed *edgeways*, stretching up and away, and presenting to his gaze only a narrow line.

If he wished to see more, he would have to travel away from the equator, south or north, to a position where he might gain a sideways view of the Rings — not merely of the lowest, but of the great width of all three, extending upward. Then, indeed, if other circumstances, such as the sunlight falling in the right direction on them, were favourable, he would see something!

Beginning at less than six thousand miles from the planet — or from its cloudy envelope — lies the Crape Ring, so called from its transparent nature. It reaches upward for nearly eleven thousand miles.

Then comes a gap, and after it, another Ring; the Inner Ring, a very bright one, reaching up and up for another eighteen thousand miles.

Then a second gap, over two thousand miles wide, followed by a third Ring, the Outer One, eleven thousand miles wide; still always reckoning the width as upward and away from the planet.

We on Earth have, in telescopes, a clear view of these Rings, lying one outside another, when we happen to be in the right position. But at times, when we happen to be — not, like the supposed man, just under them, but actually just over them — then we, too, see them simply as a faint line, hardly visible.

What are these Rings? What are they made of?

They were once believed to be actual rigid Rings, solid and fixed, revolving as a whole round the planet. But this was proved to be impossible. The tremendous pull of that great world, acting on a structure part of which lay so near and part so far away, must long ago have broken it up.

What now is believed, and is accepted as practically certain, is that they are formed of countless multitudes — millions of millions of millions — of tiny bodies, which whirl incessantly at tremendous rates of speed round Saturn, each in its own separate orbit. Practically, each one is a minute satellite, living its own small life like any other satellite.

But imagine what must be the enormous numbers of them, to make the Rings visible to us at this immense distance. Think, too, how great the speed, if it can prevent them from falling down on the body of the planet.

No doubt the partial transparency of the inner Crape Ring is brought about by the small bodies not being so plentiful — not so crowded together — as in the outer Rings.

This theory about their make has gained remarkable support through the spectroscope. Not only was it found that the different Rings did not travel all together at the same pace, as they must have done were they one solid structure; but also, the *parts* of each Ring nearer to Saturn went faster than those more distant, and these, again, revolved more rapidly than the outermost portions.

In fact, each part of each Ring went at the same pace which would have been taken by any ordinary satellite, revolving at just that distance from the planet. This once and for all settled the question as to their being each one a solid and complete whole.

It is thought not at all unlikely that, once upon a time, other planets — if not all of them — were loose masses or clouds of tiny particles whirling in company around the Sun, and that gradually, as centuries and millenniums passed, these particles drew closer together, forming masses, and in time taking shape as worlds. It may have been thus. If so, Saturn's rings will perhaps in time draw together in a like manner, the nearer parts joining the body of the planet, while more distant parts might possibly coalesce into "moons."

Saturn, therefore, at his present stage, may be actually a younger member of the family than Jupiter, not so far developed.

Yet the thought brings perplexity; for no signs have been seen of the violent hurricanes and perpetual tornadoes which seem to rage on Jupiter, caused, no doubt, by the great heat of that planet. Saturn appears to be in a more quiet condition than his tempestuous twin; hot enough to keep his oceans aloft in the form of dense clouds, though perhaps — this is only conjecture — perhaps no longer a scene of furious storms and whirlwinds. But why it should be so is a mystery, seeing that Saturn is the lighter in make, which would seem to imply a less cooled condition.

In any case, and even if he really is cooler and less turbulent than his comrade in the skies, Saturn can hardly be looked upon as ready to support any kind of animal life known to us, so long as his waters still float in his atmosphere as steam or vapour.

Uranus and Neptune are probably more or less going through the same stages of development as the great twins.

> "Not from the stars do I my judgment pluck,
> And yet methinks I have astronomy,
> But not to tell of good or evil luck,
> Of plagues, of dearths, of season's quality;
> Nor can I fortune to brief minutes tell,
> Pointing to each his thunder, rain and wind,
> Or say with princes if it shall go well,
> By oft predict that I in heaven find."
>
> SHAKESPEARE

PART VIII

OUR SOLAR SYSTEM

I. - MUTUAL INFLUENCES

THE system, of which our Sun is head and ruler, vast in comparison with our Earth, yet small in comparison with the Universe, must not be pictured as a piece of fixed and rigid mechanism. On the contrary, both as a whole and in all its parts, it is in perpetual motion. From the center to the outskirts, it is never for one instant at rest.

To make this clear, recall the various movements of Earth and Moon.

First: the Earth spins incessantly, day and night. Second: the Moon spins on her own axis, and travels round the Earth once every month. Third: both Earth and Moon journey round the Sun in close company once in the course of twelve months. And fourth: both Earth and Moon wander through space on a vast and mysterious voyage, travelling with the Sun and all the other planets and satellites.

Viewed in the first and second of these aspects, we can talk of the Moon as *our* Moon. But viewed in the third and fourth, she is a planet, just as our Earth is a planet.

As truly as Earth is under the Sun's dominion, so also is the Moon. Both are so heavily pulled by the Sun that both would rush towards him and would drop down on his fiery surface, were it not for the vehement impetus and the strong outward pull of their own swing around him. This outward drag of rapid motion just serves to balance the inward drag of his attraction.

In addition, the Earth has a powerful influence over the Moon, so powerful as to keep her small friend always near. But when we speak of the Moon as going round the Earth, while the Earth goes round the Sun, we do not state the matter fairly. Earth and Moon travel in company, each controlled by the Sun, and each more or less affected by the other.

The Earth's journey is far from being a smooth and even line, since she is constantly swayed, not only in a tiny fashion by the weak attraction of the Moon, but also by the pull of any passing planet. And the Moon is far more irregular in her advance, because, from her light weight, she is so much more easily drawn this way and that way.

So her orbit really is a complicated affair, since it is at one and the same time a pathway round the Earth, a pathway round the Sun, a pathway through space, and a pathway perpetually affected by the influence of her neighbors. This last is true also of all planets.

As she swings to and fro in a series of bends or scallops round and with the Earth — not in *loops*, but in *curves* — she is now on one side of us, now on the other, now between us and the Sun, now on the farther side away from the Sun, continually changing her speed to fit in with the forward or the backward pull of the Earth. But all the time she is compelled to press steadily forward on her true main pathway round the Sun, if she would not be dragged down upon his blazing surface.

And as Earth with her Moon journeys round the Sun, so Mars with his two tiny moons, and Jupiter with his ten, and Saturn with his ten, and Uranus with his one, and Neptune with his four, travel in their orbits. All these other moons are influenced by their "primaries" and by their companion-moons, hurried on or drawn back, from time to time, on their various orbits. So each member of the family has power to help or to hinder other members.

A fresh thought comes in here. As above said, our Earth has two distinct forward movements: first, round the Sun once each year; secondly, onward with the Sun through space. And this means that *she never once in all the ages, so far as we can tell, comes back to any earlier position in the heavens.* Though she does travel round and round the Sun, and though we talk of the "plane" level of her pathway, it is not strictly a "plane" at all.

For the Sun himself is traveling onward and upward — if we may speak of "upward" where no "up" or "down" exists, except as arbitrarily named by us on our little Earth. Still, from our point of view, north of the equator, his peregrination with his family of planets is upward.

Therefore also the journeying of our Earth really is, not a perpetual circling round and round on one level, but a corkscrew-like advance in a ceaseless spiral. And this, which is true of our Earth, is true of all the planets of our Solar System, and probably of all other planets in the Universe. It is true also of the Moon, with an addition; for her monthly circling round about the Earth is in itself a spiral advance, and her journeying as a planet around and with the Sun is another spiral — a journey of the same description, only on a larger scale, ever onward to fresh realms and "pastures new" in the wide domains of space.

> "Thou, O Sun,
> Soul of surrounding worlds; in whom best seen
> Shines out thy Maker, may I sing of thee?"
> JAMES THOMSON (1700–1748)

> "Thou, proud man, look upon yon starry vault,
> Survey the countless gems which richly stud
> The night's imperial chariot. Telescopes
> Will show thee myriads more, innumerous
> As the sea-sand.
> Now, proud man — now, where is thy greatness fled?
> Less, less than nothing."
> HENRY KIRKE WHITE (1785–1806)

II. - THE POWER OF ATTRACTION

Somebody may ask: But *why* does the Sun pull at the planets? And why do they all pull one another?

To this "why" we can only answer that so it is. Just as our Earth pulls at every body on or near her surface, so each body in all the wide heavens draws each other body towards itself with a never-ceasing pull. A large, heavy body like the Sun drags powerfully. A small, light body like the Moon draws feebly. But one and all — with no exception, and including even the smallest meteorite — they do it.

The actual strength of the pull in each case depends not only on weight, but also on nearness. The closer two bodies come together, the harder is the pull of each for the other. The Sun drags more at Mercury than at Venus; more at Venus than at the Earth; more at Mars than at Jupiter; more at Saturn than at Uranus.

To meet this added pull, those planets which lie nearer to the Sun have to whirl round him much faster than those lying farther away. Mercury flies along at a pace of thirty-five miles each second. Venus finds twenty-two miles a second sufficient. Our Earth does eighteen miles a second. Mars needs no more than fourteen miles each second. The big outer worlds are much more deliberate. Jupiter moves only about eight miles, and Saturn only about five miles, in one second, while Uranus and Neptune creep along their distant pathways at four and three miles each second.

Not really very slow, even the last-named, if we consider that Neptune journeys at a speed three times as fast as an express train. It is only slow when compared with the rush of other worlds.

This mysterious force of attraction, or gravity, or gravitation — so called because things *gravitate* or *draw together*—is found in action throughout the entire Universe.

But what that force is in its nature, and precisely how it works, no man living can say. It *seems* to be everywhere at once. Distance *seems* to offer no impediment, no hindrance. It may possibly take time to travel, even as light does; but if so, the speed must be so tremendous as to lie, at least thus far, beyond our reach. The most delicate of measuring instruments has had no success here.

Besides worlds and their attendant moons, other bodies of less importance belong to our System; one and all under the control of this same gravity; one and all needing to be ever on the rush, if they would escape destruction.

These other members of the family are some very large, some very small; absolute opposites in size and in shape, yet closely connected. They are Comets and Meteorites.

A very ordinary notion of a comet is of a star with a long tail. But a comet is not in any sense a star, and it may or may not have a tail. More usually, the tail only comes into existence as the comet nears the Sun, arriving from a great distance. When the visitor travels away again, the tail gradually diminishes in size and finally disappears. The "starry" part is the densest portion of the whole, and even that is very light in make. It is called the "nucleus."

We have noticed more than once how the larger bodies are often the lighter in make. Here we have one of the very largest, which is also one of the very lightest. Comets are flimsy to a degree in their structure.

The head, or nucleus, may be a hundred thousand miles in diameter, and the tail may stretch away for tens of millions of miles. Yet the whole of that vast body is so thin and fragile in texture that, at the very least, five hundred thousand such comets might be needed to outweigh the Earth.

It is no longer feared that the coming of a comet may mean the destruction of our world. One might as well expect that a cloud settling on a mountain peak would destroy that mountain. Not very long ago, it was believed that the Earth, during two hours, had been "immersed in a comet's tail." But nobody was the worse for that experience; nobody discovered the fact from any personal sensations.

A comet's pathway round the Sun is usually much more "eccentric," that is, much more oval in shape, than are planet pathways.

Many small comets travel on "short distance" orbits, taking only a few years to do their little journeys. Others go much farther off, into the regions of the big outer planets. The famous one, which is named after "Halley," travels as far as Neptune, and its return happens only once in seventy years.

But others take such distant voyages into outer space that even Halley's Comet is, by comparison, a "stay-at-home." These restless members of the family return to the neighborhood of the Sun, not in the course of seventy years, but in the course of hundreds of years, and in certain cases, it was reckoned that the wanderers would need a million years to complete their circuits. Think what a voyage that must be — how long and dark and slow, through the greater part of the way!

Shall we try to follow one, not quite so long? Take one that needs only four hundred thousand years for its journey, and picture in your mind a very, very long, and very, very narrow orbit, not like the planets' orbits, nearly round, but so drawn out that the two sides seem all but parallel. Only at each end, the sides curve round and meet, and within one end, very near the end, is the Sun.

Then, picture the comet — without a tail — plunged in distant space, so far away, so close to the further end or loop of that long orbit, that it cannot hope to get back to light and warmth in much less than two hundred thousand years — earthly years, I mean.

Yet still it is under the Sun's control — a small and far-off Sun whose drawing power holds it in leash and keeps it from breaking loose and wandering away forever. Even yet, though it seems to be lost in outer darkness, that drawing power, ever so gentle but ever in action, does, in time, make itself felt.

Through nearly two hundred thousand of our years, the comet has been going farther and farther and farther from the Sun, from light and warmth, but always with slackening speed. And now it is almost at a standstill. Slowly, it rounds the outer loop of its long and dreary journey, and then, at a crawl, it begins its return.

Year after year, century after century, he is coming back, coming through icy chill and blackness, yet *coming*; moving slowly but always with increasing speed as the pull of the Sun grows stronger, till at length the wanderer passes the orbit of Neptune, then that of Uranus, then that of Saturn, then that of Jupiter.

And as it comes, it grows a tail of wonderful size and beauty, a tail which streams behind it for perhaps tens of millions of miles. Or it may have two or three or many tails, and these will undergo curious

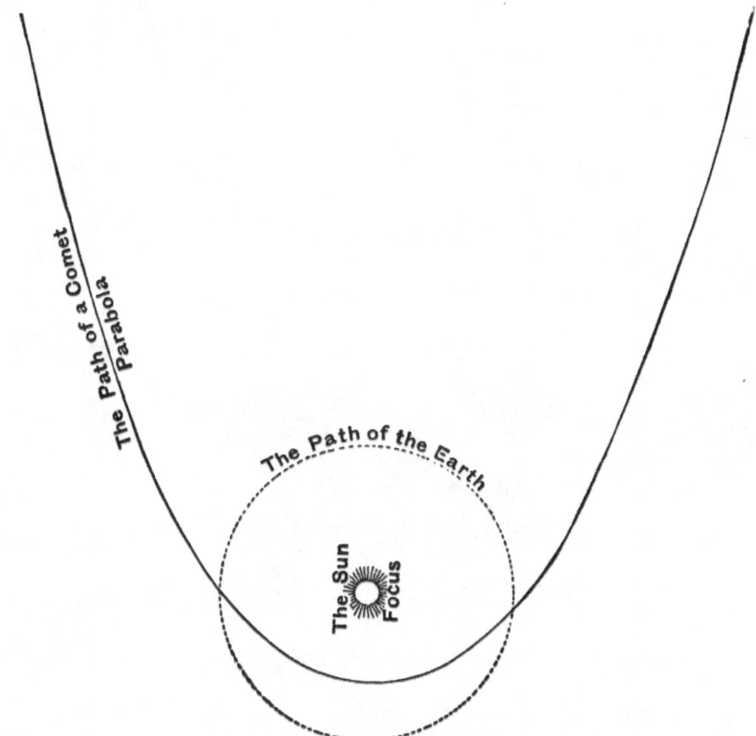

ORBIT OF A COMET, WHICH WANDERS OFF NEVER TO RETURN

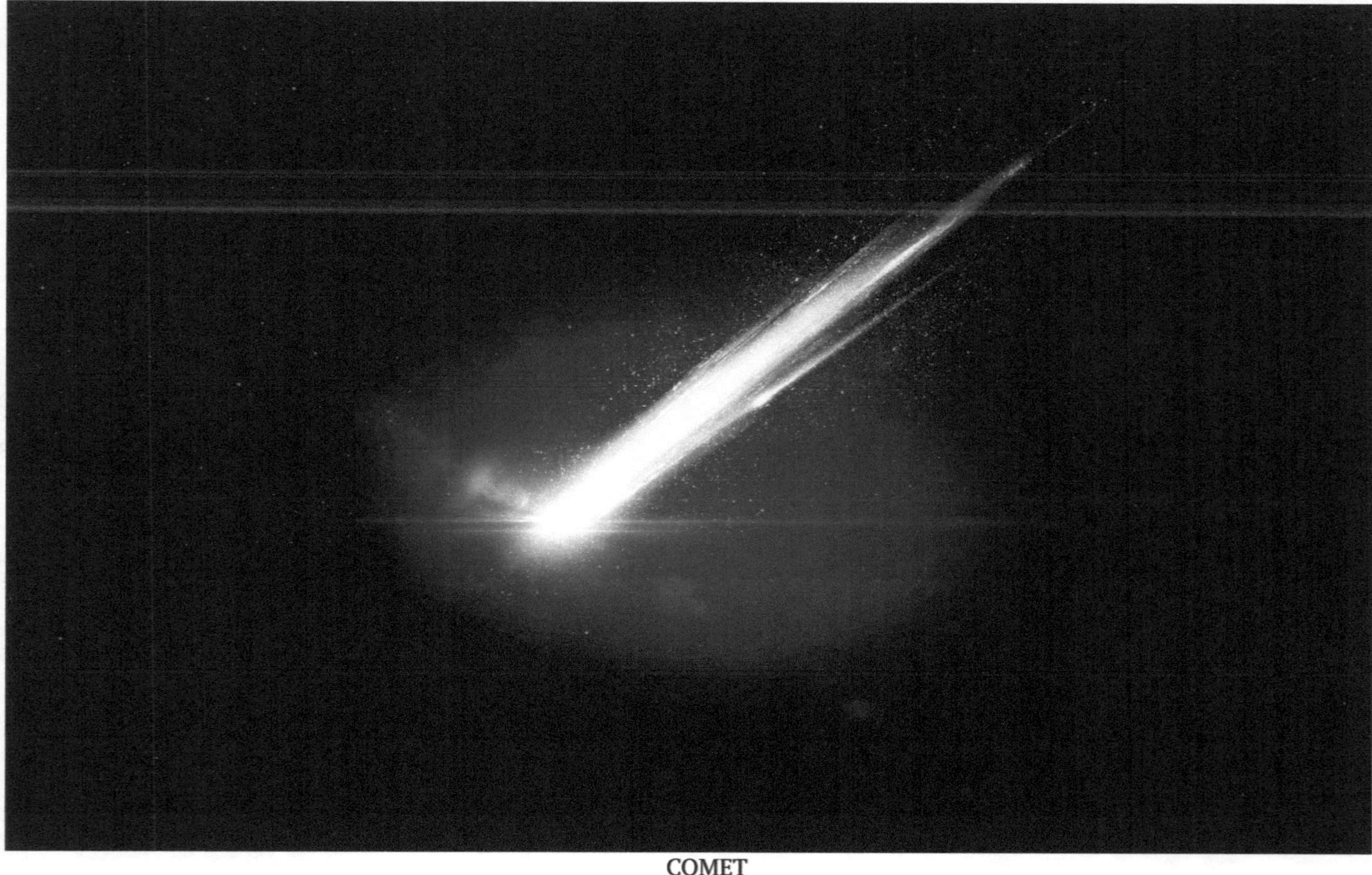

COMET

changes of form on the way. Its speed becomes a rapid rush, swifter than the pace of any of the worlds, for it draws nearer to the Sun than the nearest of the planets.

At last, in a magnificent fling, it whirls round the narrow curve, going at a terrific rate, and its tail swings round also, pointing all the time right away from the side of the Sun. It once more begins its retreat, wandering away and away for another two hundred thousand years, into realms of utter darkness and icy cold, going ever more slowly, as the Sun's pull lessens with distance. And while it thus travels, its tail now goes first and the head follows after, and gradually the tail itself disappears.

Such, in brief, is the story of certain comets belonging to our System. There are others which perhaps do not so belong; or, if they once did, they have broken loose from the Sun's control. So great is their speed that not all his drawing power can hold them. They pay a passing visit and wander off, never to return.

It is believed that the Sun exercises a curious repulsive power over the tails of comets, driving them always outward and away from itself; and it has been suggested that possibly this repulsion may reside in light.

> "That very law which moulds a tear,
> And bids it trickle from its source,
> That law preserves the earth and sphere,
> And guides the planets in their course."
>   SAMUEL ROGERS

A word of explanation here as to the curious "streaks" on the comet photograph. They really are stars. The telescope, traveling with the surface of our Earth, and moved by clockwork to counteract that motion, is steadily fixed on the comet, thus taking its "likeness" during a more or less long exposure. But the far-off stars, lying at great distances beyond, are left behind by the moving telescope as it follows the comet and are "as it were dragged across the field of view, leaving each one a trail of light on the photographic plate." This is not seen in a photograph of a nebula; for the nebulae are, roughly and as concerns the telescope, on the same *plane* as the stars, whereas the comet, when photographed, is enormously nearer, probably either within or not very far from the limits of the Solar System.

III. - ROUGH ORE OF THE UNIVERSE

Some little way back, a connection between comets and meteorites was mentioned. We have now to think about this connection.

And first — what *are* meteorites?

If present theories hold good, they are the rough ore of the Solar System, and indeed of the Universe; the "raw material" out of which suns and worlds, satellites and comets are fashioned.

A meteorite, such as those that have been found to have fallen on the Earth, may be of any size, from a mass of iron or other solid substance as big as a house, down to balls no bigger than a cricket ball, or a marble, or a pea, or even a grain of sand — though by that time we are getting down to meteoric dust.

The head of a comet is believed to contain, or to consist of, masses of meteoric iron, large or small. The tail probably contains or consists of nothing more substantial than the finest meteoric dust; specks of matter floating widely apart, each reflecting the Sun's rays. In addition to this, comets very likely shine in part by their own light.

Meteorites in enormous numbers — numbers beyond calculation, beyond imagination — exist throughout the Solar System; and hundreds of them are perpetually falling hither. When one happens to wander so near as to be captured by Earth's pull, then, as the small body rushes earthward, the friction of our atmosphere heats it intensely, making it glow with a brilliant light.

If we happen just then to glance in the direction of its rush, we see what looks like a star flashing along in the sky and vanishing. But it is not a star. It is only a captured meteorite.

In less than a second, during which it may have traveled twenty miles or more, the small body has ceased to shine because it has ceased to be. A tiny shower of dust drops quietly down, and that is the end of the "shooting star."

Once in a while, if the meteorite should be unusually large, part of it reaches the ground as a solid and very hot lump. But this comes to pass so seldom, in comparison with the numbers which simply disappear, that we can only suppose the big specimens to be very few as compared with the small ones. At all events, it seems to be so in those parts of the sky where our Earth journeys.

Such a solid body arriving here is called an Aerolite, and aerolites have been often found to be largely made of iron. Some of them may once have formed part of a comet's head.

At certain seasons of the year, we touch on streams of meteorites, and see many more shooting stars than in other months; and now and again, at long intervals, our Earth has passed through a vast horde of these little bodies, plunging into the midst of them as a swimmer might plunge into a shoal of fish. A grand sight has then been witnessed. Thousands and thousands of bright meteors were watched, hour after hour, flashing and dying in the heavens.

Meteorites are believed to congregate in countless myriads of legions, around and about in the neighborhood of the Sun; and the Zodiacal light, seen at times from Earth, is supposed to consist entirely of them.

So too, as we found earlier, do the Rings of Saturn — millions of millions of little bodies ever whirling round that great world, and journeying with him round the Sun.

Moreover, it has been thought that the Earth and all her brother- and sister-worlds were once upon a time masses of loose meteorites, held together by their mutual attraction, and gradually, slowly, through ages, drawing closer and closer together, as they passed from stage to stage on the road to becoming solid. This was mentioned a little earlier, and we have had glimpses of those successive stages in the history of Saturn, of Jupiter, of Mars, of Earth, of the Moon.

But one great example of an intermediate stage, between the loose condition of separate meteorites and the seemingly liquid condition of Saturn, has not yet been brought forward. That is the *Sun-stage*.

It may well be that the raw material, out of which has been fashioned this Solar System — Sun, Moon, Earth, planets, satellites, comets — at a certain stage of development consisted simply of meteorites. But this does not bring us anywhere near the beginning of things. Tracing back from small solid meteorites, we come to fine meteoric dust, of which comets' tails may be largely composed, and vast quantities of which probably exist throughout our whole System. And that fine dust, traced still farther back, would no doubt land us amid enormous masses of slowly revolving gases. And beyond the gases — who can say what next?

But all such theories should be taken cautiously and held lightly. In speaking of the far-past, we do not *know*; we can only conjecture. In the end, they may prove to have been right theories, or they may have to give place to other explanations.

PART IX

DISTANCES AND MEASUREMENTS

I. - A REDUCED SCALE

To bring before our minds a clearer notion of what is really meant by the distances of our Solar System, we will try now to picture the whole on a smaller scale, less difficult to grasp than the real figures.

You still have to think of the whole family belonging to our Sun as one great system, but as lessened everywhere throughout in size, while keeping just the same *proportions*, each with respect to the rest.

So we will let ONE INCH stand for ONE THOUSAND MILES, both for sizes and for distances. Thus, two inches will mean two thousand miles, three inches will mean three thousand miles, and so on.

All the planet-distances given here are *from the Sun*, not from the Earth. We take the Sun as the center, which he is, and reckon outward from him, counting our Earth for what she actually is — one small world among many, and not in size even one of the most prominent.

First, we must have the Sun, a radiant, blazing body about seventy feet in diameter. Picture a large ball, dazzlingly bright, as high and as wide every way as a good-sized house. And each inch in its height, breadth, and entire make stands for one thousand miles.

Mercury, a small ball three inches in diameter, travels round the Sun at a distance of five-ninths of a mile.

Venus, nearly eight inches in diameter, travels round one mile away.

Earth, matching Venus in size — with her Moon about twenty feet off — travels round at a distance of one mile and a half.

Mars, only four inches in diameter, two miles and one-fifth away.

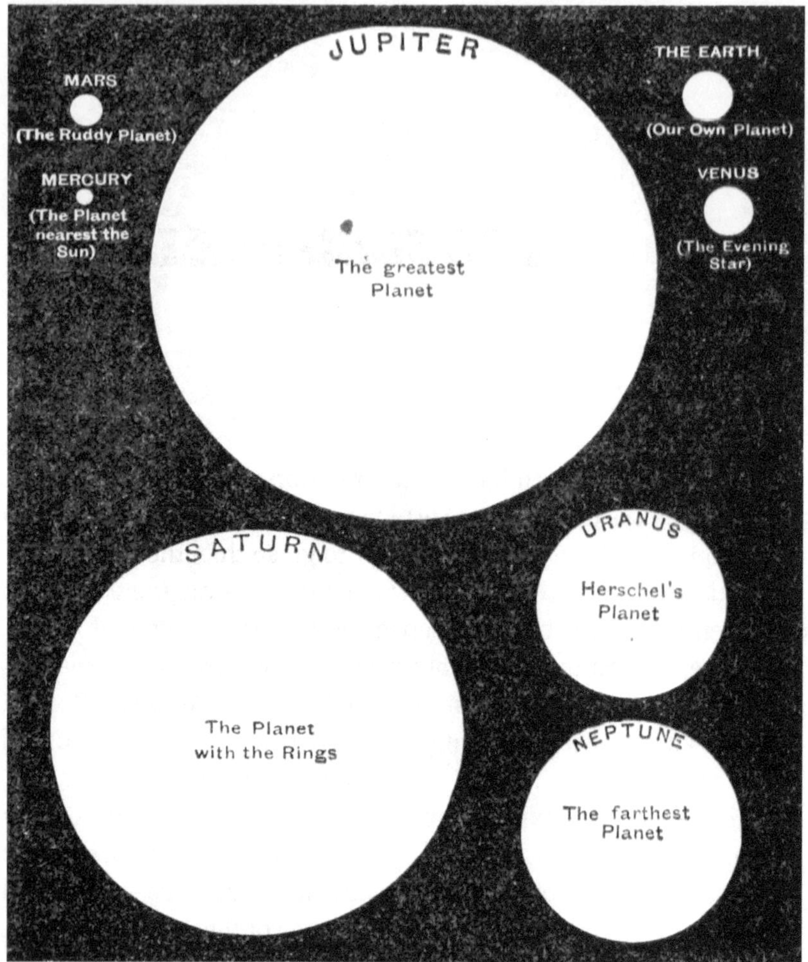

COMPARATIVE SIZES OF THE CHIEF PLANETS

Then a considerable company of very minute Minor Planets, scattered round in a belt, to which most of them keep.

Jupiter comes next — a big globe, seven feet in diameter, journeying round at a distance of seven miles and a half from the Sun.

Saturn, six feet in diameter, on an orbit fourteen miles from the Sun.

Uranus, thirty-two inches in diameter, twenty-eight miles distant.

And Neptune, thirty-five inches in diameter, forty-three miles away from the Sun. For all his seventy feet of diameter, that Sun by this time will have sunk to a very small object.

The whole Solar System, thus reduced, one inch standing everywhere for a thousand miles, would be contained within a circle of about one hundred miles in any direction. Some of the comets alone would travel outside this limit. The diameter of each planet-orbit, that is, its breadth across from one side to the other, is twice the distance of that planet from the Sun. So Neptune's whole orbit would measure some eighty-six miles across, well within the hundred.

Picture it to yourself, this reduced Solar System — all these little balls, some so tiny, and none but the central Sun larger than seven feet in diameter — floating at wide distances one from another, each keeping to its own pathway. And in the empty spaces between, nothing — except an occasional comet, and countless hordes of tiny meteorites.

But when we have compressed the whole Solar System in this manner, till it all lies within a circle one hundred miles in diameter — what of the STARS?

What, indeed, of them? Where do they come in? Our Sun is the one and only star included within the bounds of the Solar System. All the others lie outside. And the question for years, for centuries, was how far off did they lie?

Briefly, on this scale, one inch standing always for one thousand miles of real distance, how near will be the very nearest star in all the heavens — the very nearest yet known to us?

That star would have to be placed at a distance from the hundred-mile circle of the Solar System of FOUR HUNDRED THOUSAND MILES, or not much less than twice *as far as the Moon actually is from Earth.*

Few indeed come anything like as near. Others, viewed on the same scale, would have to be placed at distances of five hundred thousand miles, six hundred thousand miles, and far more. And still, each inch of those dividing spaces would represent one thousand miles of real distance.

Does this give some faint idea of the immensity of our Universe?

II. - ANGLES AND TRIANGLES

But how can we possibly know all these sizes and distances? How can men, living on our little Earth, be able to make them out? Is it all guesswork?

Certainly, it is not guesswork. No tape has ever been carried to the Moon. No plumb-line has ever been dropped upon the Sun. Yet we can say how far away they are, for those distances have been measured.

And measurements of objects in the sky — of their distances from us — are carried out in much the same mode as measurements here on Earth of distant objects. A man on one side of a river, unable to cross over, can find out its width. Surveyors have constantly to do this kind of thing, to make such calculations. From one side of a river, they can estimate the distance of a tower far beyond it, and also the height of the tower.

Such measurements, one and all, it may be said, are founded on ANGLES.

We all know what an angle is. When one straight line, coming towards a second straight line from a slanting direction, meets it, there at once is an angle. Draw two straight lines on a piece of paper, making two of the ends meet, and again you have an angle. Then draw a third line, joining the two separate ends of the first two, and you have a triangle.

Triangles may be of many shapes. The three sides may be all exactly equal. Or the one side may be short, and the other two long.

This can be varied to any extent by further shortening the short line and lengthening the long lines.

Suppose you are on an open plain, with clear views all around. A little way in front stands a pole, planted in the ground. Note very carefully, from where you stand, against what part of the landscape that pole seems to lie; against a tree, or a house, or aught else. Then walk several paces to right or left and note again. It no longer lies against exactly the same background. Your own real change of position has caused an apparent change — a slight "shifting" on the part of the pole.

From where you first stood to where you moved is a straight line — your BASE-LINE. A base-line is most important in all such measurements, whether earthly or heavenly. From each end of this base-line, another line is carried by your eyes straight to the pole, and the two lines meeting there form with the base-line a triangle. If the pole is near, and your base-line is fairly long, a short and broad triangle is the result; but if the pole is distant, and your base-line is short, it will be a long and narrow triangle.

You may test this for yourself with different objects: with a sapling, with a tower. Note in each case the "shift" of the object, due to your own movement from one end to the other of your base-line, and see how the shape of the triangle changes with the increased shortness of the base-line, or with the increased length of the other two lines. Try it in the open; and then try to work it out, ever so roughly, on paper.

A certain word — "parallax" — is much used in astronomy with regard to the distances of heavenly bodies. In a dictionary[11], the meaning of this word is given thus: "The apparent change of position of an object relatively to other objects when viewed from different points; the difference between the place of the Sun, Moon, or a planet, as seen from the Earth's surface and its center at the same instant." So your experiments will show you, with earthly objects near at hand, practically the same thing that in astronomy is known as the "parallax" of a planet or a star.

But how can this small "shift," this seeming displacement, be of

11   The Student's English Dictionary.

any real use in finding the distance of anything, either on Earth or in the skies?

In a little book of this kind, it is hardly possible to enter fully into the question; indeed, a complete explanation could not be given without an amount of technical language and mathematical demonstration, by means of diagrams, which, even if I could undertake to work it out thoroughly, would not be welcomed by the greater number of my readers. However, perhaps it is possible to offer a general notion of the main principle that lies at the foundation of such measurements.

Now, place two sticks precisely upright in the ground, just one yard apart. That yard on the ground is your base-line. Suppose that those two sticks could be lengthened out and out indefinitely — carried on and on upwards into the sky — how soon would the two tips meet and touch?

Never! If they are perfectly straight in themselves, and if they are placed perfectly upright, and if they continue upwards with absolute straightness, never deviating by the thousandth part of a hair's breadth - then they would go on side by side, always one yard apart, for miles, for hundreds of miles, for thousands of miles, for millions and billions of miles. They would never meet. To the end, they would still be just one yard apart.

But suppose that, as you fixed them in the ground, you gave them a careless little *tilt* each towards the other. Would they then go on always apart?

No. Sooner or later, they must touch. How soon would depend on how much you had made them slant at the first. They might meet in two or three yards, or in a hundred yards, or in half a mile. From the length of your base-line — exactly one yard — and from the angle at each end of it, one who understood the right method might reckon roughly about how far off that meeting spot would be.

The Moon is much farther away than any tower or hill on Earth. There is all the difference between possibly one or two hundred miles and over two hundred thousand miles. To discover the Moon's distance from any ordinary base-line was found impossible. So a new plan was devised. Two stations, widely apart, were chosen. Astronomers at these two places made each their observations of the Moon's exact position in the sky and compared notes.

That plan proved a success. The Moon's parallax could finally be measured, and calculations made. Time after time, with ever better instruments, it was undertaken until now we know accurately how far away from us she floats.

But the same scheme with the Sun was a failure. From a position ninety-three million miles away, it would not work. Not even a baseline eight thousand miles long was enough to cause any "shift" of position on his part. Other plans had to be tried, and the first to meet with real success was by means of the "transit of Venus." The passing of that small planet across the brilliant face of the Sun gave a chance that was eagerly seized when once it was known to be a possibility.

Here, again, observers were planted in two places, as widely apart as the size of our Earth permitted, having between them a base-line nearly eight thousand miles long. Each had to note with extremest care, first, the instant when that tiny dark body was just within the Sun's outer edge — "limb" is the correct word — and also the exact instant when it just quitted the further edge. And here at last was found the shift of position, not shown in the position of the Sun himself, but in the tiny difference of time noted by the two observers, so widely parted, in the moment of Venus passing between Earth and Sun.

You understand, of course, that on these rare occasions — only twice in a century — Venus is no nearer than usual to the Sun. She merely passes exactly *between* Sun and Earth, so as to be seen *against* him. And from the minute difference in time of these apparent "touchings," as seen from opposite ends of the base-line, the Sun's distance could be reckoned.

III. – BUT — THE STARS?

Then came the question of star-distances. If the Sun lay nearly one hundred million miles away, how far off might be the fixed stars?

For this great problem, the diameter of our Earth proved useless. It had been tried and tried in vain. It was far too short a base-line. Not a star stirred in response. Not the faintest sign of a "parallax" could be seen. And no possibilities existed here of any other heavenly body crossing the face of a star, for no star in all the sky has a "face" for us, except our Sun. Each to our sight is a point only, with no breadth, no disc.

A grand idea came up. If the diameter of Earth was as nothing in respect of star-distances, what of our yearly journey round the Sun? What of Earth's two positions in mid-summer and mid-winter? Would not that give a base-line long enough to make even the stars show a "shift" in their positions? Twice ninety-three million miles — a tremendous base-line, this.

And it was tried. Close and careful observations were taken at one date of several stars, and six months later, when the Earth was about one hundred and eighty million miles away from where she had been at the date of the first observations, these were repeated.

Failure again! Not a star seemed to stir. Not a single shift, however minute, could be detected. Not one hoped-for parallax was found. Even that enormous base-line sank, it appeared, to but one point in relation to the stars.

It was desperately disappointing. But astronomers would not despair. Again and again, they tried this plan — for indeed no other was known — with more and more delicate instruments. And at last, they were rewarded. At last, one star here, another there, did show a very, very minute shifting of its position; a very, very tiny seeming displacement, due to Earth's huge change of place.

From these slight results, the distances of a few stars could be roughly calculated. Not, of course, with anything like exactness, but enough to be real and dependable.

Only a few, among the thousands and millions seen. With by far the greater number, no stir becomes visible. Many more have been measured since that date, yet the great majority of them lie beyond our reach.

Still, it is something to know, even roughly, how far, how very, very far away, even the nearer ones lie; how vast is the dividing chasm which separates us from the tens of millions — probably the hundreds of millions — of blazing suns of which our wonderful Universe is composed.

You may perhaps say that I have not really explained the manner in which such calculations are worked out. No; for that I fear you must go in for mathematics and for trained teachers, who will carry you through such preliminary instructions as are necessary before you can enter into the whole question. All that I have attempted to do is to give you a slight foundation idea of the gist of the matter, to make you see how it has been approached. If you have vision enough to gain a glimmer of what these calculations really mean, you will at least see something of the wonder — not only of the actual knowledge gained, but also of the minds of those men who, in the first instance, grappled with such stupendous difficulties and overcame them. The *results*, won by their tireless courage and perseverance, may be mastered by those who have had no technical training, and in this little book, my aim has been to give, simply and clearly, many such results.

It may be of interest, if I add, with regard to this question of base-lines and triangles and "shifts," that you yourself are perpetually acting after the same mode.

When you judge the distance of anything that you see — as you do, mechanically, and for the greater part unconsciously — *you* are using a base-line and triangles. The space between your two eyes is your base-line, and the object at which you look, whether near or far, is seen by each eye in a slightly different position — against a slightly different background — from that in which it is seen by the other. Your two eyes combine the two views, and your brain at lightning speed works out the problem and gives you the result.

If you had only one eye, you would not have that base-line. But you could carry out the same plan by first looking with your one eye, and then moving your head, so as to take a second view with the same eye, much as when astronomers observed the stars from one position in Earth's yearly pathway round the Sun, and six months later observed them again from another. The principle in both cases is the same.

In thus judging by sight, we are by no means always successful. Much depends on natural aptitude, and much also on practice. Look at an aeroplane passing overhead, and make a guess at its height above the ground. You are all but certain to give an estimate very wide of the mark.

But those who are constantly in practice may arrive at an extraordinary accuracy of judgment. I have just come across the following statement, with regard to British anti-aircraft gunners in the war: "Archie gunners will tell you at a glance the exact height of any machine flying over their position[12]." These men had used to good purpose their natural powers.

In finding out the *sizes* — the diameters — of heavenly bodies, the Sun, the Moon, the planets, variations on the method above described are followed. The general principles underlying are the same.

> "I will fear you, O Stars, never more.
> I have felt it! Go on, while the world is asleep,
> Golden islands, fast moored in God's infinite deep.
> Hark, hark, to the words of sweet fashion, the harpings of yore!
> How they sang to Him, seer and saint, in the far-away lands;
> 'The Heavens are the work of Thy Hands;
> They shall perish, but Thou shalt endure;

12   Four Years in the Royal Flying Corps, by J. T. B. McCudden, V.C.

Yea, they all shall wax old —
but Thy throne is established, O God, and Thy years are made
    sure,
They shall perish, but Thou shalt endure —
They shall pass like a tale that is told.'"

JEAN INGELOW.

PART X

OUR OWN GREAT SUN

I. - ONE AMONG MANY

FROM worlds we pass now to STARS — to bodies so intensely heated as to shine by their own intrinsic brilliance, not merely with reflected light.

Some years ago, in a certain address given in public by a well-read man — only, not well-read on astronomical subjects — a very curious assertion was made. "Put out the Sun," the speaker said, "and all the stars will cease to shine."

It was difficult to believe that he really meant what he said. But again and again, with added emphasis, he made the same statement, till it became impossible to question his intention.

If he had said, "Put out the Sun and all the *planets of the Solar System* will cease to shine," he would have been quite right. For the planets depend, entirely or mainly, on the Sun for their shining; but the stars do not so depend. If you could, by any possibility, "put out the Sun," his worlds and moons would sink into darkness, becoming invisible, except perhaps for a very faint light from the big twins, visible at no great distance. But the stars would not vanish from our sky. They would remain just as bright as they were before.

Many people, as I have had to say earlier, find an odd difficulty in distinguishing between stars and planets. Again and again they are told that stars are suns, and that planets are worlds; and still their confusion of mind goes on.

Yet really the distinction is not so very hard to grasp, and the seeing of it is needful to any sort of understanding of the heavens.

Another speaker I can recall, who made a no less astounding remark. "When you see a lovely Moon, and all its stars circling round it," he said, and how he carried on the sentence I have forgotten. That was enough.

We may kindly hope that by "circling round" he really meant "encircling." In a sense, one may suggest that the stars seen round about in the neighborhood of the Moon at any particular time do perhaps seem to "encircle" it, though in no sense can they be said to "circle round" it. But "its stars" is a phrase absolutely without sense. No stars in all the heavens can be said to belong to our tiny Moon.

Our Sun is a star, brother to all those twinkling points which lie scattered over the sky; and each separate star, so far as we can tell, is in its measure a sun, larger or smaller, brighter or dimmer, than our Sun. True, some suns *may* gradually, in the course of centuries or millenniums, change into worlds, parting slowly with their heat, becoming cool and dim, but perhaps still warmed and lighted by some other near and more powerful sun. But so does a boy change into a man; so does a sapling change into a tree; yet we do not confuse the meaning of "boy" and "man"; of "sapling" and "tree."

Of all those glittering points that we see, not one, you may be sure, is a world, such as our Earth or Venus, such as Jupiter or Saturn.

Any number of such worlds may indeed be there, in those profound depths, scattered among the stars, perhaps traveling around and with one or another of them, as the planets of our Solar System travel round and with our Sun. But if it be so, we cannot see them. Not even the most powerful of our telescopes can show to us their dim shining. The light of a world, which is only borrowed, not intrinsic, is far too faint to cross the enormous chasm of space which lies between us and every single star in the sky.

Every single star — except one! As we pass from worlds to stars, we must begin with the nearest star of all, with the one and only star in the Universe which can in any sense be spoken of as "near" —with our own "bright, particular star," the great and glorious Sun.

TOTAL SOLAR ECLIPSE

"A pleasant thing it is for the eyes to behold the Sun," truly wrote a wise man of olden days; and few would be found to differ from him.

We have seen how poets love to write about the Moon, and the Sun also has come in for their attention, though perhaps they more often prefer his sunset beauty to the full glare of noonday. As when Wordsworth wrote —

> "The Sun, that seemed so mildly to retire,
> Flung back from distant climes a streaming fire,
> Whose blaze is not subdued to tender gleams,
> Prelude of night's approach with soothing dreams."

Or Miss Procter —

> "There I have seen a sunset's crimson glory
> Burn as if Earth were one great Altar's blaze."

Or Longfellow —

> "The day is done; and slowly from the scene
> The stooping Sun upgathers his spent shafts,
> And puts them back into his golden quiver."

II. - THE SUN'S MAKE

Our Earth is not so dense and hard as the cold and rigid little Moon. Jupiter is not so dense and hard in make as our Earth. Saturn is less dense than Jupiter. And the Sun is very much less dense than Saturn. In actual age — apart from length of existence — we may rank them thus. The Sun is very young and unformed. Saturn, though much more advanced, is still extremely juvenile. Jupiter is distinctly older. Our Earth may be looked upon as middle-aged, and the Moon as decrepit.

A good deal has been said already about the comparative sizes of Earth and Sun; but another illustration is worth giving.

Suppose you could put a very long piece of tape right through the Sun, from his north to his south pole. Having so done, you may use that same tape, which gives the diameter of the Sun, to measure round the outside of Jupiter and of the Earth. It would fold *three times* round Jupiter, with a good length to spare. And it would fold more than *thirty times* round the Earth.

Here is one more proof of the Sun's huge bulk. Imagine placing our Earth inside and exactly at the center of the Sun. Imagine that the Moon is still traveling round and round the Earth, at her present distance of two hundred and forty thousand miles. Not only would the Earth and the Moon and the whole circle of the Moon's pathway round the Earth be inside the Sun, but beyond that circle would lie a belt, two hundred thousand miles wide, still within the Sun.

You must not, however, picture to yourself the Sun as a hollow globe, able to afford space for an Earth and Moon in any such wise. Still less may you think of him as a cool, firm, solid globe. He is singularly light in make, weighing less in proportion to his size than even Saturn. This fact is easily explained by another fact, that he is tremendously hotter than either Saturn or Jupiter; therefore the particles of which his great bulk is composed are looser — lie farther apart — and so the weight is less.

Like the planets, he spins steadily on his axis, doing the turn in about twenty-six days. Parts of the surface move more rapidly than other parts, so that at the equator the time is as just stated, while farther north or south it is twenty-seven days. This alone shows that the surface of our Light-giver cannot be fixed or stable.

We saw that Jupiter was fairly hot. But on and around *this* radiant globe, the heat must be awful beyond words, beyond imagination; surpassing infinitely the fiercest furnace heat and glare ever known on Earth. That vast and raging atmosphere, instead of being made like our atmosphere of cool gases, contains metals floating aloft as glowing vapors, metals which with us are in their ordinary state cold and hard.

No metals there are as we have them here — not even iron. Neither cold nor solid, nor even liquid, they are all gaseous, all in a condition of furious heat and turbulent wildness.

Much of what is known about the Sun has been learned through the spectroscope; that wonderful instrument which breaks up beams of light from Sun or star into strips of color, and whispers the meanings of those color-bands, and of strange little dark lines found in them, for human beings to read and to translate.

No one has ever looked through the Sun's outer envelopes into the depths below. Once upon a time it was imagined that *perhaps* a cool and firm body lay within, that *perhaps* even a safe and agreeable dwelling-place for beings like ourselves might be found there.

Such dreams have been long given up. The Sun's interior is now held to be formed throughout of furiously heated gases, possibly near the center so highly compressed under the overlying weight as to be denser than water and in some ways like a liquid, or even like a solid; but certainly not from coolness.

The whole body seems to be wrapped in an envelope or enclosing shell of extreme brilliance, called the "photosphere" or "sphere of light." Its actual nature is one of the problems not yet settled. Till lately it was believed to consist of radiant clouds, not formed like earthly clouds of condensed water-mists, but of condensed metallic vapors. But this view is now seriously questioned. So tremendous must be the heat, it is doubted whether metals known to us here could possibly be condensed under such conditions, and would not remain gaseous. Time and further research will, we hope, show the true nature of the photosphere, and whether it is formed of anything like metallic clouds.

Outside the photosphere comes the next envelope — the "chromosphere." During a total eclipse, when the radiance of the photosphere is cut off, all around the dark body of the Moon is seen a wonderful, quivering rim of fire, from which spring often sharp red heights. This rim belongs, not to the Moon, but to the Sun. It is a vast ocean of glowing gases, clothing the whole body of the Sun, though we can see it only at the edge or "limb"; and it is probably many thousands of miles in depth.

And outside the chromosphere lies the wide and lovely corona, stretching far in all directions, and constantly varying in shape. It is supposed to be made partly of gases, and partly of vast masses of meteoric dust, shining by reflected sunlight, and also perhaps partly by its own light arising from intense heat.

Whatever the photosphere really consists of, it gives out a blinding glare, which, even at a distance of ninety-three million miles, is a danger to human eyesight. What must it be like there — or halfway there? And these clouds, and the crimson ocean above, and the gaseous atmosphere over that, all whirl and rage and storm perpetually in such tornadoes and cyclones as we on our quiet little world cannot in the faintest degree imagine. The wildest hurricane ever known here would be as a bubble in a teacup, compared with the least and mildest of solar outbursts.

A singular *mottled* appearance is often observed on the surface of the Sun; sometimes described as looking like rice grains scattered lavishly.

But for the help given by a total eclipse, we might never have known of the red ocean of fire, or of the beautiful corona. They can now be examined, even when no eclipse is going on, by means of the spectroscope; but they were first discovered through observations at the time of an eclipse.

An eclipse of the Sun is caused — not, like an eclipse of the Moon, by the Earth passing exactly between Sun and Moon, but — by the Moon passing exactly between Sun and Earth. The little Moon, being so near to us, while the huge Sun is so far away, just suffices for a very short space to hide or nearly to hide the whole Sun. Sometimes only a part of the dark body of the Moon crosses over only a part of the bright body of the Sun; but sometimes we have what is called a total eclipse. Yet even then, though the dazzling face is completely veiled, the rim of crimson stands out just beyond the Moon's dark covering body; and out of that ocean of fire are seen to spring vast prominences or "flames" usually invisible to us. These prominences are clearly shown in the two illustrations.

III. - SPOTS AND "FLAMES"

All that we see, commonly, when we give a glance at the Sun, is a round and dazzling face, too dazzling to be safely examined without smoked or tinted glasses. If we did carefully thus examine that surface, we might possibly catch a glimpse of one or two tiny dark spots.

For the Sun is often spotted, and frequently with spots large enough to be made out by the naked eye. Men were very long discovering this fact, which perhaps shows how seldom they could have taken the trouble to observe with real care.

It was by means first of these spots — small as we see them, but by no means small in reality — that his turning on his axis became known. They were watched, travelling across the bright disc, taking ten or twelve days for the journey, then disappearing behind, and in about another twelve or fourteen days reappearing on the opposite side. For though they are not permanent features, they often last for a considerable time, changing their shapes indeed to a certain extent, yet not so much that they cannot be easily recognized, even after many days of absence.

Like the "bands" of Jupiter, they are usually found only within a certain distance north or south of the equator. Whether they sink deep into the Sun's surface has been a question much discussed. The more general view now seems to be that they are, in all probability, shallow, possibly almost flat. But they are often enormous in extent. One huge specimen, seen in February 1905, was described as covering

TOTAL SOLAR ECLIPSE

"*more than four thousand million square miles.*" Our small Earth would not go far towards filling up that hollow — if it be a hollow!

Mention has been made of "sharp red heights" springing from the crimson ocean of fiery gases which clothes the Sun. They are generally called "prominences," and sometimes "flames" or "sun-flames," as already explained.

In size, they are extraordinary, not as to flat extent, but as to height. Like spots, they may last for many days, and have even been recognized as reappearing after absence. It is only possible for us to see them when they are on the rim — the "limb" — of the Sun, standing out against the sky. We then have a view of them sideways, instead of looking up at them from below. As the Sun incessantly turns round and round, each part of his surface in succession is at the edge. So for two or three days, they become visible, standing out, and then they vanish, perhaps to reappear later on the opposite edge.

The number seen at any one time varies. Sometimes they are very few; sometimes as many as twenty or thirty may be there. In height, they differ much. More usually they range from about twenty-five to eighty thousand miles, but monster prominences are observed, very much beyond this. A French writer recently described them as "gigantic eruptions of flame, ten times, twenty times, fifty times higher than the whole diameter of the Earth."[13]

Frequently, the upward rush of these glowing gas masses has been watched from Earth. And while some continue for at least a week or two, others are startlingly rapid in their growth, and short in their existence. Such outbursts, like earthly cyclones, may be either slow and lasting or rapid and soon over. But we can hardly speak in the same breath of our infantile tornadoes or whirlwinds, side by side with the tremendous eruptions on the Sun.

These Sun-flames were mentioned in a chapter on the Moon, as being so lofty that, if our Earth were as near to the Sun as she is to the Moon, one of them might at any time leap out and engulf her. And this is literally true.

Towards the close of the last century, a prominence was watched

13   *L'Astronomie*, September 1919, p. 9.

TOTAL SOLAR ECLIPSE
PORTION SHOWING PROMINENCE

by Professor Young, rising to a height from the Sun's surface of *three hundred and fifty thousand miles*. Compare that with the distance of the Moon from us.

When speaking of the "surface" of the Sun, you must not picture to yourself any solid or liquid surface. It is only such a surface as exists with great masses of vapour or gas.

A remarkable prominence was seen and photographed in May 1916, one photo following another, recording its changes. It rose rapidly to a tall column, which curved over, and at first parts seemed to be falling back on the Sun. Then these were seen to be fresh streams rising, and presently the main column broke up. All this happened between about 8:50 a.m. and 9:20 a.m. But even later, some faint "wisps" could be detected at a height of nearly half a million miles above the Sun.

And we must remember that these wonderful outbursts, seen only at the edge, may be perpetually going on all over the Sun.

One thing is clear: that both they and the spots are in their natures different forms of furious tornadoes or cyclones or stormy upheavals of fiercely heated gases of one kind or another. Certainly, the dark tint of the spots does not mean more than *relative* coolness. White spots also are seen and photographed; and they, too, no doubt are raging storms of some description.

What a different globe we have in the Sun, from the Moon! - All fire and glow and tempest, in place of cold and serene stagnation.

The whole of our heat and practically the whole of our light come to us from him. Moonlight is reflected sunlight. Planet-light is reflected sunlight. The brightness of the sky, the flashing of ocean waters — these are borrowed from the Sun. Without him, we should be in darkness; colours would exist for us no longer; grass and trees would not be green, the sea would not be blue.

If the Sun's heat were banished as well as his light, ours would be a frozen world. Almost all our warmth we owe to him. Artificial burning is produced through the heat given out, whether in the past or the present, by him. The very coal that we burn is, as has been said, "bottled-up sun-heat"; and our lamps, our candles, our gas, our electricity, one and all depend on his work.

If our Sun were removed to the distance of the very nearest "fixed star," every living creature on Earth would die. Our oceans would become solid masses of ice, and a ceaseless winter-night of appalling cold and blackness would everywhere prevail.

> "The grey-eyed morn smiles on the frowning night,
> Checkering the eastern clouds with streaks of light
> And flecked darkness like a drunkard reels
> From forth day's path, and Titan's fiery wheels:
> Now ere the Sun advance his burning eye,
> The day to cheer, and night's dank dew to dry,
> I must up-fill this osier cage of ours,
> With baleful weeds, and precious-juiced flowers.
> O mickle is the powerful grace, that lies
> In herbs, plants, stones, and their true qualities:
> For nought so vile that on the Earth doth live
> But to the Earth some special good doth give;
> Nor aught so good, but, strain'd from that fair use,
> Revolts from true birth, stumbling on abuse."
>   SHAKESPEARE: ROMEO AND JULIET

PART XI

A BROTHERHOOD OF STARS

I. - SUNS AND THEIR PLANETS

ALL that our Sun is to his company of worlds, other suns may be to their worlds, if or when they have any. Such far-distant worlds probably exist, and possibly in myriads, though we cannot see them.

A man standing somewhere near any star in the sky that you like to name — one can hardly suggest his standing *on* a star! So perhaps I should rather say, any man floating in space near a star — if he still had eyesight such as ours — might be able to see our Sun. But it would be as a star only, a bright or dim star, according to his distance. And he would not be able to make out a single planet belonging to our small System. No glimmer from Jupiter or Saturn, still less from Venus or Earth, could affect the retina of his eyes.

So it is not in the least astonishing that we on Earth cannot detect any of those far-off worlds which, we can hardly doubt, must belong to at least some among the radiant Brotherhood of Suns.

Sirius, the brightest star in all our sky, was known through ages as a solitary orb. And though in later years a companion to him has been discovered, faintly shining and revolving with and about him, that companion can only be another star, much cooler and probably a good deal smaller than himself, as well as far more dim; yet still a sun; not a planet or world. No mere world, shining by borrowed light, could possibly be seen by us at such a distance, even with the help of a most powerful telescope.

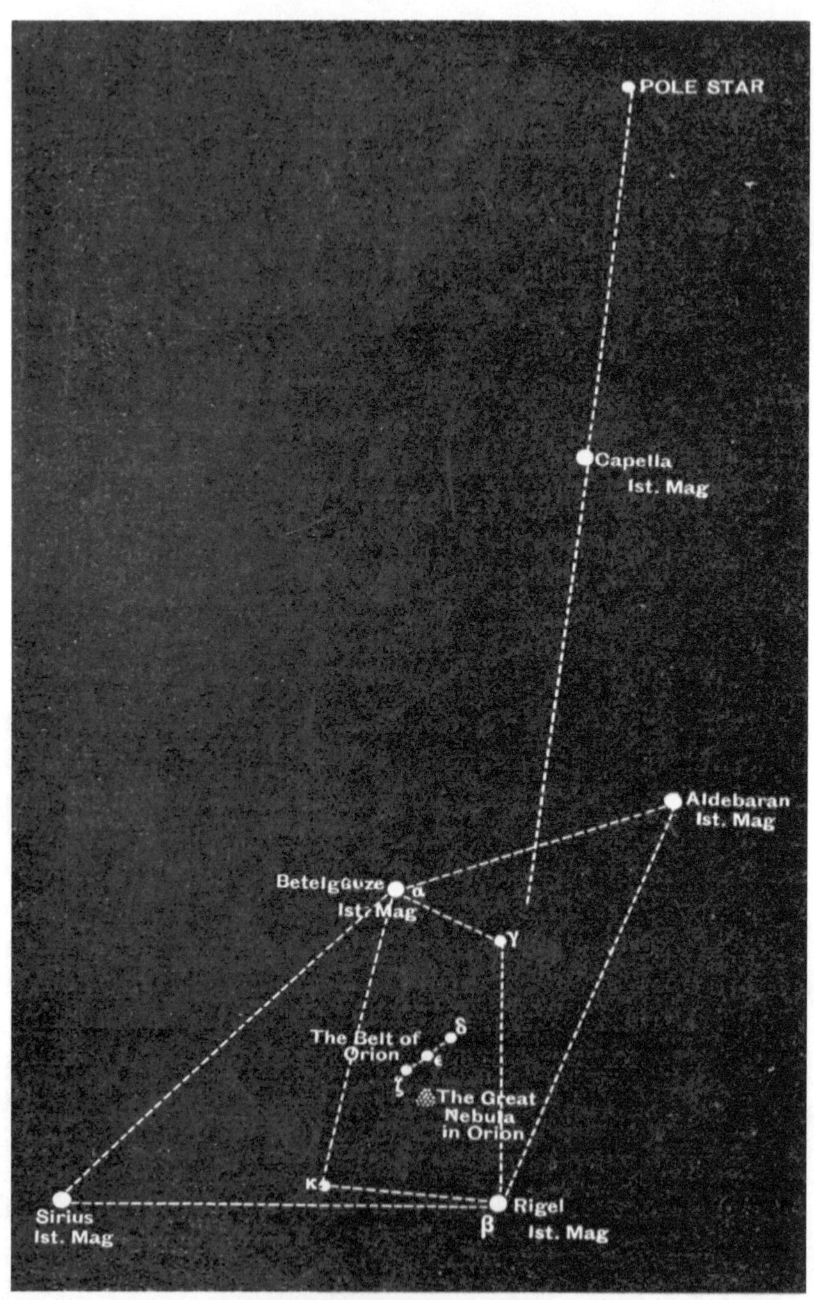

POLE-STAR, ORION AND SIRIUS

But those two suns, the brilliant Sirius and his paler friend, *may* have any number of planets journeying around and depending on them, even as the planets of our System journey around and depend upon our Sun. Vega and Capella may have their worlds. Arcturus and Aldebaran may be centres of systems. So may any or every star which helps to make up the Pleiades group, or the Constellations of the Great Bear, the Little Bear, the Southern Cross, Orion, or any other collection of suns in the heavens.

Many stars, once believed to be single as was Sirius, are now known to be double. Instead of travelling alone, like our Sun, surrounded only by inferiors, two suns journey in company, one of the two being usually larger than the other, and both revolving round one centre. In some systems, three suns are found; in others, four; in others, many suns.

Such facts — and they are facts, not mere conjectures — seem to open out wonderful possibilities for living beings who might reside there. We can imagine planets floating amid many radiant suns, where no night could ever be known, probably no bleak winters ever be felt, because light-givers and heat-givers would be on every side.

This, however, is conjecture. We do not know that such worlds exist, or that, if they do, they have any inhabitants. And strong doubts have been expressed whether such conditions would really result in desirable dwelling-places; unless, of course, the inhabitants are expressly adapted to their surroundings, which, on the whole, we might with good reason expect to be the case!

All these countless stars in our sky, or at least the great majority of them, are SUNS, more or less like in make to our Sun. They, like him, are vast, blazing furnaces of heat and light. They, like him, have their radiant photospheres; their glowing and enfolding oceans of fire; their stormy and furious atmospheres of brilliant gases; no doubt also their raging cyclones and mountainous prominences.

These things we know. Once again the spectroscope steps in, and breaks up the slender strip of light which has travelled from a star, and tells us some of the secrets of its construction, even whispering what kinds of minerals float as glowing gases in that star's atmosphere.

It sounds like a wild dream, does it not? But it is no dream, no fancy.

"I could not sleep for thinking of the sky,
The unending sky, with all its million Suns,
Which turn their planets everlastingly
In nothing, where the fair-haired Comet runs.
If I could sail that nothing, I should cross
Silence and emptiness, with dark stars passing;
Then in the darkness see a point of gloss
Burn to a glow, and glare, and keep amassing,
And rage into a Sun, with wandering planets,
And drop behind; and then, as I proceed,
See his last light upon his last moon's granites
Die to a dark that would be night indeed;
Night, where my soul might sail a million years
In nothing, not even Death, not even tears."[14]

14   From *Lollingdon Downs*, by John Masefield. Pub.: William Heinemann. By permission.

II. - VARIETIES OF STARS

In the whole Universe, probably, no two stars could be found exactly alike, any more than on Earth two leaves or two grass-blades are seen precisely the same in shape or in markings.

Infinite variety prevails there, as everywhere in Creation. Dull uniformity is no part of the Divine plan. Stars are no more "equal" than human beings are "equal." There are great stars and small stars, swift stars and slow stars, brilliant stars and dull stars. "Star differeth from star in glory."

Many attempts have been made to sort these countless suns in classes. One plan followed was that of classifying them by colour — Red Suns, Yellow Suns, White Suns, and so forth. A more recent suggestion rests mainly on size — Giant Suns and Dwarf Suns being the two chief classes proposed. Many stars, however, must belong to a doubtful borderland between the two.

Among the varieties of stars known to us, are — Double Stars, Variable Stars, and Temporary or New Stars.

Herschel was the first to discover true Double Stars, and the earliest alighted on by him was looked upon as a great marvel. Others soon became known, and very large numbers now, not to speak of Trebles and Quadruples, are familiar objects in the sky for astronomers. Till telescopes revealed their secret, these were all looked upon as single stars.

Variable Stars do not shine always with an unchanging brightness.

Many of them go through steady and regular vicissitudes, in short or long periods.

For instance, Algol, belonging to the constellation of Perseus, is generally a star of nearly the second magnitude. But once in the course of every three days or so, it fades away to the lessened shining of about a fourth-magnitude star, stays thus for some twenty minutes, then reverts to its ordinary condition.

Mira Ceti, another "Variable," takes a longer time. It may be seen as a second-magnitude star. Then, during some months, it fades slowly, till it becomes invisible to the naked eye, and continues to lessen long past that stage, after which it gradually rallies. These changes last through a good part of a year. Mira Ceti was the first of the kind discovered—whence the note of "wonder" in its name.

Others belonging to this class are much more uncertain and eccentric in their behaviour.

In many cases, such as that of Algol, where the alternations are regular and comparatively brief, it is known that the cause lies in the presence of a second dim sun, revolving round or with the first, thus passing from time to time between the star and us, and so diminishing its light. But this explanation does not serve with the more irregular Variables.

Temporary, or New Stars are extremely interesting. From time to time in the history of our world, a sudden new star has blazed out in the sky, often with startling suddenness. The star itself may not be actually "new," in the sense of never having been observed before, but its radiance is new. It becomes very evident that something unusual and unlooked-for has happened in that far-off sun, tidings of which have only just arrived here.

Two remarkable new stars have already appeared since the dawn of the twentieth century: one, Nova Persei, or the new star in the constellation of Perseus, in 1901; the other, Nova Aquilae, or the new star in the constellation of Aquila, in 1918.

Nova Persei was first noticed in February 1901, and it made a very abrupt appearance. One night earlier, a photograph of that part of the sky had shown no trace of a star just in that spot. Yet here it was, a bright star of the second magnitude, and by the 23rd of the month, it already outshone some of the first-magnitude stars. From this great brilliancy, it gradually lessened, though not without many ups and downs, as if from time to time the outburst — of whatever nature it might be — broke out afresh, again to lessen. In the course of two years, it had sunk to a star of the tenth magnitude.

Nova Aquilae, in 1918, was first observed on June 8, already bright. In two days more, it outshone Vega, and was said not only to be brighter than Nova Persei, but to exceed all previous new stars since 1604. It too faded gradually, though not without some "flarings-up" by the way, till it had become a somewhat variable star of the tenth magnitude.

Many possible causes for these sudden appearances have been from time to time put forward. For a while, the one more generally accepted was of a probable collision between two heavenly bodies. The clashing of vast streams of meteors has also been suggested. It is now thought more likely that the tremendous outburst — and tremendous, indeed, that outburst must be to become visible to us at such an enormous distance — may be due rather to the blazing up of extensive masses of gaseous matter surrounding a star. What brings about that blaze is not so easy to say.

Many stars are largely gaseous in their makeup, and they are often surrounded by immense envelopes of nebulous matter or far-reaching atmospheres of gas.

New stars are usually found in the regions of the Milky Way, where distant suns seem to congregate far more densely than in our part of the heavens.

"Ye stars, which are the poetry of Heaven."
BYRON

III. SMALL WAVELETS

One of the most amazing things in the universe, and indeed, throughout the whole of creation, is light — what light is and how light travels.

A ray of light is not everywhere at once. It is not simultaneously at the Sun and here on Earth. Light journeys, and at a great pace. Its rate of advance is - *one hundred and eighty-six thousand miles each second.*

You know our Earth's diameter. Well, the journey of a ray of light in one second is equal to a flash backwards and forwards through the Earth, from and to England and Australia, between eleven and twelve times! Rather difficult to picture in one's mind!

The farther away any body is from us, the longer a ray takes to reach us. Sent from the Moon, it arrives in one second and a quarter. From the Sun, it takes eight minutes and a quarter. From Jupiter at its nearest, it takes slightly more than half an hour, and at its farthest, just under an hour. From Neptune, the journey takes four hours. And from the nearest star, light takes over four years.

So here again, by light measurement as by measurement in miles, we encounter the great gap of emptiness surrounding our Solar System on all sides before another star is found.

A light ray, when undisturbed, always travels in a straight line. However, if it strikes a body of any kind, it glances off to one side or the other, at an angle depending on the slant of its strike. This is similar to when a rubber ball is thrown against a wall; it will glance off to the right or left according to the direction from which it is thrown. If it arrives directly from in front, it will rebound towards the spot from which it was thrown.

But Light is not a solid body, like a ball. It is generally held to be the result of enormous numbers of tiny waves - or vibrations - not of air, but of that delicate and subtle *something* called ETHER, which we believe fills all space throughout the Universe. Though we cannot, through sight or through feeling, be conscious of its presence, we are sure that *something* is there, acted upon by light, for the tiny wavelets have been closely studied, measured, and counted.

Their numbers and their speed are extraordinary and beyond imagination, with many billions arriving in just one second.

The Universe must be a magnificent tangle of star beams, crossing and mingling in all directions, as millions of suns emit their countless billions of light rays moment by moment. Once started, all these rays journey onward and ever onward, always at exactly the same speed and in straight lines unless disturbed by an obstacle in their path — continuing to the furthest limits of the starry universe, and perhaps farther still.

But though the rays actually journey onward as tiny wavelets of ether, they are not visible as light to human eyes. Space itself, through which they travel, is - so far as we are concerned - in darkness. Each ray is hidden, till it meets with a check. Then it shines forth.

This makes one think of the hidden and undeveloped powers sometimes unexpectedly found in a man; perhaps in one of placid and easy-going nature, not given to greatly exerting himself for others. Suddenly comes a check - a shock of some kind - and at once the hidden powers, the undeveloped force, the unsuspected spirit of self-sacrifice, till then dormant, shine forth. Have we not seen something of this with many in the Great War?

IV. - THE NATURE OF LIGHT

Mention has been several times made of the spectroscope. And though in these pages I cannot attempt to give any adequate account of that wonderful instrument, it is perhaps worthwhile to offer once more a slight foundational idea, lying at the root of what it accomplishes for us.

A ray of light may be said to come to us as a strand of many-coloured threads, not opened out, but rolled or woven into one. And the spectroscope unrolls or unravels this strand, flattens it out, spreads it forth for our inspection. Then the threads of which it is composed lie side by side.

Great things are often built on the same principles as little things, and rare matters on the same foundations as everyday matters.

The "bow in the cloud," though not "little," is a very ordinary and everyday affair, not in the least astounding, because we are so used to it. Yet that rainbow really means a ray of sunshine opened out, spread forth, showing the lesser sub-rays of various colours, which, when bound or woven together, make a single ray of white light.

A like result may be brought about with the use of a piece of glass shaped as a prism. If a ray of sunshine is allowed to pass through a very narrow slit into a darkened room, and a prism is placed in its path, the prism will break up that entering ray into its separate parts, throwing on the floor or wall a row of lovely colour-bands. These bands range, like the colours in a rainbow, from violet at one end to red at the other end. And all the bands of delicate colours are a consequence of innumerable billions of tiny wavelets, which have travelled as a ray of white light from the Sun.

The numbers of ether wavelets which strike the eye differ with the colours. At the red end of the scale they are bigger and slower; and *only* about four hundred and fifty billion of them arrive each second — a billion meaning one million millions. But at the violet end, they are smaller and more rapid, and their numbers rise to eight hundred billion each second. With other colours, lying between the red and the violet, the numbers vary between these extremes.

This "scale" is what can be seen by human eyes. Other "notes," so to speak, lie above and below, and take effect in various ways, such as invisible heat and photographic rays; but we human beings cannot *see* them, though we can feel the heat and can use photography.

What the prism actually does is sharply bend the sunlight-ray out of its straight path. And since the sub-rays, of which it is made, are not alike in their composition, some are diverted more and some less, so that they lie side by side on the wall or on the floor, instead of remaining all bound together in a single ray!

A spectroscope may be made with two or many prisms, used in complicated ways. But what it did in the first instance, and what it does still, was and is to tear up or dissect a ray of sunlight, thus giving what is called the Sun's "spectrum."

Such results of a ray of light being passed through a prism had been long known and long viewed with interest. But in the beginning of the last century, a fresh discovery was made, at first an extremely puzzling one. The "solar spectrum" — that row of colour-bands which is sometimes now spoken of as a "keyboard of light" — was found to be crossed by mysterious *fine dark lines*, running up and down through the bands.

Only three or four of these lines were seen at first. Then, with closer observation, more and more could be detected, till it was known that hundreds of them — nay, thousands — were there, perpetually there in a ray of sunlight. And they did not change. Whenever a sunlight-ray came under examination, those same lines were found, always in the same positions.

Different kinds of prisms were used, and the lines were still there. Moonlight was tried, and the lines were still there. Light coming from the planets was tried, and the lines were still there. Then the light from certain stars was put to the test, and this time those particular lines were no longer there. Black lines indeed were found, but not now the precise number and the precise arrangement seen in the Sun's spectrum.

Do you see the point of this? The Moon and the planets shine by reflected sunlight, so they could only give more feebly the Sun's spectrum! But the stars shine by their own light; therefore, each star has its own particular and individual spectrum, unlike those of all other stars, and unlike that of the Sun.

We might almost say that the spectrum of each star is its own private signature. Each especial star in the sky has its own private *signature*, distinct from that of every other star.

Something else came up for consideration.

Any kind of metal here on Earth, if it is sufficiently heated, if it is made white-hot or is further melted into a liquid, and if its light is made to pass through a very narrow slit and through a spectroscope, will give a spectrum of colour-bands.

But if the metal is heated very much more, so that it becomes a *gas*, then there are no colour-bands, but instead *bright lines* are seen; different bright lines for each different metal. These bright lines, again, may be called the "signature" of each metal. No two are exactly alike.

Sodium — one of our commonest substances — under such conditions gives, among others, two bright lines, close together; these two are always in exactly the same position on the "keyboard" of colour. Iron, under the same conditions, gives a great many bright lines, always arranged in a particular way.

Here was the clue, yet some time passed before it was used.

One astronomer did notice a curious likeness between the pair of sodium lines and two dark lines in the Sun's spectrum, but he went no farther. Then the idea was taken up by another astronomer, and he tried a very interesting experiment.

First, he obtained a sunlight spectrum, not a very strong one, but just enough for the two dark lines to be visible. Then he put, between the narrow slit and the sunlight, a flame in which sodium vapour was burning. At once the two dark lines vanished, and in their place shone two bright lines — the lines of burning sodium vapour.

So far he had used only softened sunlight. To make assurance doubly sure, he now allowed a full stream of radiant sunshine to pass through the sodium flame into the slit. And instantly, the bright sodium lines disappeared in their turn, to be replaced by the pair of black lines!

That the two were actually one — the pair of bright lines and the pair of dark lines, both showing the presence of sodium gas some-where — could no longer be doubted. It had been a question simply which of the two was the stronger; which could overcome the other. Each in turn triumphed.

This same experiment he tried again and again with other metals, finding with each in turn the same result. The bright lines given, for instance, by glowing iron vapour, hundreds in number, were exactly reproduced by dark lines in the Sun's spectrum, just as with the pair of sodium lines.

It was a remarkable discovery, showing that in the Sun, and also in many of the stars, the very same substances which we have on Earth exist as gases or vapours. It really meant that the bright pair of lines, the signature of sodium gas, said: "I am sodium on Earth;" the dark pair chiming in with, "And I am sodium in the Sun." Or, again, that the hundreds of bright iron lines proclaimed, "We are iron on Earth;" the dark lines responding, "And we are iron in the Sun."

But, you may ask, why should the lines be sometimes bright and sometimes dark?

Because in one case something comes between. The bright lines arrive directly from the burning sodium or iron vapour. But such rays, arriving from glowing sodium gas or iron gas in the atmosphere of the Sun or of a star, have on their way to pass through a rather less fiercely heated atmosphere, surrounding the Sun or the star. And in that passage, the slightly cooler sodium gas in the Sun's atmosphere robs the ray of that which would produce the double bright sodium lines, or the iron gas robs it of that which would produce the many bright iron lines. So those parts of the ray, instead of arriving here as *bright* notes in the "keyboard," come as *blanks*. It is much the same as when a musician strikes certain notes on a decrepit piano, and no sound results. The observing astronomer sees only *black* spaces in place of bright lines — very narrow, because the light has been allowed to come only through a very narrow slit. If it were widened, they would not be visible at all.

Proof after proof was found of the reality of these readings, many tests of various kinds being tried before they were finally accepted as genuine. Now we know that the spectroscope does indeed tell us, and with no uncertain voice, which metals float as glowing gases in the Sun's atmosphere, and which are also found in the atmospheres of different stars.

It does other things besides this. One in particular has to do with star-journeyings.

For a long while, astronomers could only observe and reckon the *sideways* movements of stars. Their journeyings straight towards us or straight away from us were impossible to make out.

But through a very slight *shifting* of those little black lines in a star's spectrum towards the red end or towards the violet end of the keyboard or spectrum, the "line-of-sight" journeyings of a star can be measured.

The idea at first may sound wild and improbable. It has, however, been tested again and again with movements of bodies nearer at hand, such as spots on the Sun coming nearer and going farther with the whirl of that great globe; and it has been found reliable.

V. – HISTORY IN STARLIGHT

An interesting matter in connection with starlight is its historic character.

What you and I see after dark, when we gaze at the star-spangled sky, is - the stars as they were, not the stars as they are at the moment.

Suppose you are looking at a distant street lamp. You see that lamp as it was when the ray which now strikes your eyes left it. The time between its quitting the lamp and reaching your eyes is extremely short; still, it does exist, for light takes time to make any journey. And if that lamp were put out, you would still see the flame for a tiny fraction of a second after it had ceased to shine.

Here is a ray of sunshine resting on your hand. That ray speaks to you of the state of a portion of the Sun's surface about eight minutes ago. It brings to you a photograph of what the Sun was like then, not of what it is like now.

Look at Sirius shining and twinkling in the heavens. That grand sun, which, it is said, would give us at the distance of our Sun about forty times as much light as we have now from our Sun, lies somewhere about fifty billion miles away. His light cannot arrive here in much less than nine or ten years. So the gleam of brightness which touches your eyes tells you what Sirius was like just so many years ago. It says nothing at all of what he is like at this moment.

Suppose you are looking at another star, at about the same distance; and suppose that five or six years ago a great outburst of some kind took place in that star, a tremendous flare-up of heat and brilliance. But *you* can see nothing of it. The star twinkles serenely on in our sky, just as it did about ten years ago. Not for another four or five years will it blaze forth in our heaven with unexpected radiance. Till then, all its light-rays arriving here will have started before the great event, and so they can tell us nothing about it.

Such catastrophes — if they are catastrophes — do come about now and again in different parts of our Universe. You heard of something of the kind in the account of two new stars, which have appeared in this century. Some vast outbursts must then have come about, very far off.

With the first of the two, Nova Persei, the distance was reckoned to be so immense as to make Sirius almost a next-door neighbour by comparison. One calculation gave the length of light-journeying from this Nova as not more than some three hundred years, but another spoke of about two thousand years as more likely.

If the latter estimate were correct, the catastrophe might have taken place at about the time of great events in the small land of Judaea; events on which our whole Christianity is founded. And ever since then, the light-gleams, carrying their message from the blazing orb, would have been hurrying here at the rate of six billion miles each year.

Nova Persei itself — or perhaps more truly a "nebula" of gaseous matter surrounding it—is said to have been lighted up during that outburst through an expanse probably as much as seven or eight billion miles in diameter, which would mean a space equal to about one-third of our distance from Alpha Centauri.

A sufficiently big affair, this!

One more remarkable fact must have attention here. We have already found that a ray of light travels always straight forward until it meets with a check; and by its nature, it is compelled so to do. When stopped by any solid body, large or small, from a sun or a world down to a speck of dust, it either glances off to the right or left, advancing again straight forward in the new direction, or it enters into the body, there to be broken up into its many-coloured threads or sub-strands.

This has been long known. But recently, a new discovery has been made. Light is now believed to have *weight*, which means that it is subject to attraction. A ray of light travelling from one body to another — journeying, for instance, from a star to our Earth — may on its way be *bent out of its direct path* by the pull of a solid body acting upon it.

The amount of this bending is exceedingly small. Where lesser bodies are concerned, it is so minute that to detect it at all is impossible. But when the powerful pull of a huge body like the Sun acts on a light ray, the slight curve actually can be and has been observed and measured, with the most delicate instruments.

We know how fast a ray of light travels, flashing through space at a rate of tens of thousands of miles each second. Suppose that such a ray is darting to us from one of the stars and that, on its way, it passes near the Sun. Then, the strong drag of the Sun seems to draw it gently just a little way out of its straight path, giving it an excessively slight curve. You must not imagine, however, that the star itself is any closer than usual to the Sun; for the two are still billions and billions of miles apart; only the Sun happens to lie in almost a direct line between the star and Earth. It is as if a ray of electric light, flashed to you and me from a house ten miles off, might pass closely by another house in the same direction only three miles off.

And if this is true of the light from one star, it is true of the light from all stars. Then, the countless millions of light rays, ever journeying from sun or star to other parts of the Universe, are being perpetually bent, very slightly, out of their straight paths, perpetually swayed to the right or left a very little by the ten thousand influences which affect them from suns and worlds on all sides.[15]

As our Earth pursues her annual journey, the Sun appears to travel onward; and he actually does lie against one group of stars after another. So, the rays from star after star, travelling in succession to us, bend in response to his attraction.

> "Roll on, ye stars; exult in youthful prime,
> Mark with bright curves the printless steps of Time;
> Near and more near your beamy cars approach;
> And lessening orbs on lessening orbs encroach;

15   A particular interest is attached to this fact by its connection with the new "Einstein theories," which are too complex to be gone into here.

Flowers of the Sky, ye too to age must yield,
Frail as your silken sisters of the field.
Star after star from Heaven's high arch shall rush;
Suns sink on Suns, and Systems, Systems crush,
Headlong extinct to one dark centre fall,
And death, and night, and chaos mingle all;
Till o'er the wreck, emerging from the storm,
Immortal Nature lifts her changeful form,
Mounts from her funeral pyre on wings of flame,
And soars and shines, another and the same."

ERASMUS DARWIN (1731–1802).

I. - A GENERAL WHIRL

NOT only are the stars like our Sun in their make, but also in movement. Not one individual of that radiant host is at rest. All are moving; all are journeying; all are hastening this way and that way, singly or in couples or in companies. And if they have any planets, any attendant worlds, those planets or worlds travel with them.

The speed of our Sun — which means the speed of the entire Solar System — is not very great when compared with that of other suns; or so we believe.

He travels through space at a rate of perhaps about twelve miles each second. Listen to the clock — one, two! Between those two ticks, the Sun, with the whole of his family, has gone forward *twelve miles*. And if you wish to see vividly what this means, multiply the twelve by sixty, and you will know how many miles he goes in one minute. Multiply that figure again by sixty, and you will know how many miles he goes in one hour. Multiply that again by twenty-four, and you will know how many miles he goes in one day. If you go on thus multiplying, you can discover what his speed is in miles each week, each month, and each year.

Certainly, it is not a speed to be despised when compared with earthly speeds. Yet — if this estimate of his rate of travel be correct — our Sun is by no means a particularly energetic specimen of his kind. Among other stars of the Universe, which have been closely studied, a general average pace is said to be somewhere about twenty miles each second.

But there are others which go far beyond this rate. One of the brightest in our sky is Arcturus, a magnificent sun believed to be enormously larger and more radiant than our Sun.

Though he lies at a very great distance, the speed of this sun is more or less roughly known, and it sounds terrific — a rush of *something like two hundred and fifty miles each second*. Yet, if a man kept watch year after year, he would see no change in the position of Arcturus. Only the most delicate observation, with the most accurate of instruments, could show the very, very small advance. In nine hundred years, Arcturus moves visibly across a little breadth of the sky as wide as our full Moon looks to us.

We are thinking now of *real* movements, not of any seeming shift of position caused by movements of our own. Arcturus really travels at about that rate and really moves across the sky as much as the width of the full Moon in not much less than a thousand years. Naturally, men were a good while in finding out that tiny change in his position. But does not this help to make clear what the "wide distances" of our Universe must be?

Other very rapid stars are known, though perhaps none quite so overwhelming as Arcturus, with his great size, his extraordinary radiance, and his wild onward rush. He and certain others have been named "runaway stars," yet with them, as with the rest, we find obedience to law, perfect control, and orderly advance.

Where all these suns are hastening, no man can say. Many attempts have been made to find the goal of our own Sun, with varying results. Whether the stars in general go straight forward or travel in vast curves cannot be known with certainty, at least as to the greater number.

We only know that all are on the move, that all are wending their way — somewhere! But where each one is going, and what may be the purpose of each one's journey, this is known only by Him, to Whom it could be said — "The heavens are the works of Thy Hands."[16]

Jean Ingelow wrote -

16   Heb. i. 10.

CLUSTER M. 13, HERCULIS

> "The elders of the night, the steadfast stars,
>   The old, old stars which God has let us see,
> That they might be our soul's auxiliars,
>   And help us to the truth how young we be —
> God's youngest, latest-born, as if, some spars
>   And a little clay being over of them — He
> Had made our world and us thereof, yet given,
>   To humble us, the sight of His great Heaven."

Memory recalls a curiously opposite view from that of the last few lines. Many years ago, I had gone to Oxford to make the personal acquaintance of the then Savilian Professor of Astronomy, Dr. Pritchard, after his great kindness in helping me with the corrections of my book Sun, Moon and Stars. We were speaking about the planets and their possibilities. He said thoughtfully—what led to it, I do not recall -

"Who knows? They may all be just *chips struck from the block in the making of our Earth!*"

Who knows indeed? A sculptor will ruthlessly strike away masses of marble to set free the vision of beauty which he — but no other man — already sees enshrined in a shapeless block.

II. - STAR CLUSTERS AND NEBULAE

Among the many wonders of our starry Universe, not least are the star clusters and nebulae. Large numbers of both are known to astronomers, and a certain number can be seen by the naked eye as faint cloudlets or dim and misty smudges in a clear sky.

The word "nebula" is Latin for "cloud"; and when the expression "nebulous" is used, it means "cloudy" or "hazy."

It is not an easy matter to draw an exact line between clusters and nebulae. Some star clusters can be separated by a telescope entirely into stars. Some nebulae cannot be separated at all into distinct stars. But many clusters are made up partly of stars and partly of gas masses; and many nebulae also are the same — partly stars, surrounded by vast masses of gas or "nebulosity."

One well-known star cluster in the constellation Centaur, just visible to the unaided eye, has thousands of stars packed together in a space of sky just twice the diameter of our Moon as she appears to us. Another cluster is that of the Pleiades, where, though we commonly see only six or seven stars, hundreds are really crowded among the six or seven. This does not mean that the hundreds in either case are actually "packed" or "crowded," but only that they seem so through distance. Each star in those clusters may be very far from all its neighbors.

Many years ago, it was confidently believed that both clusters and nebulae were made up entirely of stars, pressed together and rendered dim simply by the fact that they were so very far away. It was maintained that only a powerful enough telescope was needed to "resolve" them one and all into groups of distinct star points.

But though some thus yielded to increased telescope powers, others declined to do anything of the kind. And with the advent of the spectroscope, fresh tidings arrived from dim and distant regions.

For certain of these nebulae, which had obstinately refused to be separated by the telescope, were examined by means of the spectroscope; and they made a most unexpected response. In plain terms, they were requested to write their signatures, as countless other stars had done. And they did not refuse; but the style of signature came as a surprise. No soft bands of color appeared, as with our Sun and with stars in general. Only *bright lines* were seen. And this said plainly that the nebula itself must be made, chiefly if not wholly, of gaseous matter.

Among some of the best-known nebulae is a very fine one in Orion, easily seen by the naked eye. Small and dim as that hazy smudge seems to us, it is enormously large and enormously distant. Another grand one is in Andromeda; not grand as seen without help, but very much so through a powerful telescope or when photographed. Looking at a clear and good presentation of this marvel, one cannot but realize, from the curious whirlpool or *maelstrom* appearance, that the vast gas masses must surely be whirling steadily around a center. It may well be so; not with this particular nebula only. Stars are whirling; why not nebulae also, from which we believe stars and systems of stars to spring?

We have seen the Sun in his splendid youth, so much less developed than the planets or our Earth. Star clusters must be younger still, in all probability; at all events, when they consist largely of nebulous matter; and the nebula probably must take stand as yet more juvenile. Each nebula *may* be not one Sun only "in the making," but a whole system or universe of stars in embryo.

Both the clusters and the nebulae as seen by us are of many different shapes. It does not follow that, if we could approach billions of miles nearer, we should see them in precisely the same shapes.

Some clusters are globular in outline, and these are believed to be

GREAT NEBULA IN ORION

extremely rapid in movement, traveling through space at a speed of about ninety miles each second. But they are completely outdone by some of the nebulae — the spiral kind — which have been reckoned to hurry on their distant travels at an average rate of two hundred and forty miles a second.

One marked difference between stars and nebulae should be mentioned. A star is always, as seen from Earth, a *point* only, with no length, no breadth, no disc. But a nebula has a disc and can be roughly measured.

A question of no small interest has again and again come up in connection with these misty and mysterious shapes. Are they, or are they not, part of our Starry System? Do they, or do they not, belong to our Universe?

Many times in this book, the expression "*Our* Universe" has been used, and not without purpose. *The* Universe would be quite as correct; for "our" Universe is "the" one to us who live in it. But those who hear only and always of "the Universe" sometimes fail to realize that other universes may exist also, outside of and apart from our own.

It seems rather a pity that the word "Universe" has been allowed to become descriptive of one starry system by itself. The true meaning of the word, as given in a dictionary, is, "the universal or whole system of created things;" and until recent years, "the Universe" was understood to include all Creation.

Then it began to dawn on astronomers that our Starry System might not mean all Creation; and they started using the word for "ours" in particular, while other possible starry systems were spoken about as "other universes."

So now we have to speak of "Creation" or of "the Cosmos" as descriptive of all possible universes in one; though perhaps the older plan was the better.

Not far from the closing years of the last century, an idea sprang up, and was welcomed by many — that star clusters and nebulae might be other universes, far distant from our own. In which case, we had glimpses into a vast and unknown Beyond.

After a while, the thought fell into disfavor and was practically given up. Lately, it has again worked its way to the fore, more especially with

SPIRAL NEBULA M. 64

reference to the spiral nebulae. These have been looked upon by many as probably great starry systems or "universes" in the making, lying outside the uttermost limits of our Universe.

This, of course, is conjecture only; it can at present be no more, though for many minds full of interest. Yet perhaps already the pendulum has begun to swing back, and the suggestion may undergo fresh extinction or possibly another temporary banishment to a back seat.

After all, how can we know? How can we be sure? How can we even guess, with any clear prospect of guessing rightly? So great are the problems involved — so enormous the distances, even of our own Starry System alone — so unutterably vast and bewildering, aught lying beyond its limits — that, for the present at least, the question must surely rest in abeyance.

But whether we do or do not catch any glimpses of outer universes; whether our view is or is not totally circumscribed within the borders of our own; such outer universes may very probably exist. How far we can ever become actually aware of their presence is another question, not easily settled.

The Milky Way, that soft band of light which encircles the whole heaven around our Earth, is part of our Universe. It consists of innumerable stars, with clusters and nebulae plentifully interspersed. In no part of the sky do stars cluster so thickly as within and near that "Galaxy," as it is called.

You may look at one small portion of the soft "girdle" of light, and perhaps all you can see is a faint glimmer, with three or four dim stars dotted over it. But if a photograph of that same small space is put before you, it may reveal a multitudinous mass of far-off suns, crowded together, literally thousands, if not tens of thousands, where you saw less than half a dozen.

> "Look how the floor of Heaven
> Is thick inlaid with patines of bright gold;
> There's not the smallest orb which thou beholdest
> But in his motion like an angel sings,
> Still quiring to the young-eyed cherubims."[17]

17   Shakespeare: Merchant of Venice.

III. – FAR REACHING!

In an earlier chapter, an attempt was made to reduce the Solar System in imagination to a small scale, thus bringing its proportions more within the compass of our understanding. We then took one inch as standing for one thousand miles.

We will now make a much more substantial reduction, so as to view more easily the proportions of the Universe, or Stellar System, as a whole. We will take one inch as representing, not one thousand miles, but the entire distance between Sun and Earth, or ninety-three million miles.

Our Sun will be a tiny, brilliant ball, one-hundredth of an inch through, or less. This little Sun and a minute Earth — a mere speck — should be placed just *one inch apart.*

Following out the same idea, Mercury would be one-third of an inch from the Sun; Venus two-thirds of an inch; and Mars, outside the small Earth, about an inch and a quarter off. Jupiter would be five inches away; Saturn ten inches; Uranus nineteen inches; and Neptune thirty inches off. The whole Solar System could thus be enclosed in a small circle less than two yards across, leaving out only certain comets which would travel farther.

The next question is: What would be the distances of the nearer fixed stars on this scale?

If our Earth is one inch from the Sun, and if Neptune is less than one yard away, then — counting still that each inch means really

SPIRAL NEBULA M. 101 URSAE MAJORIS

ninety-three million miles — the star which lies closest of all, Alpha Centauri, must be *four miles distant.*

And between — nothing! Between that star and the little Solar System, just two yards across — *nothing*: at least, nothing in the shape of a star. An occasional tiny comet may lag along in the darkness; and dark bodies, cooled suns, *might* possibly float here or there. But of bodies radiant with heat and light, not one in all that wide area, four miles in every direction, can be found.

Astronomers sometimes talk of "stars in the vicinity of the Sun." This is what they mean by "vicinity."

Think of the distances implied. First, our whole Solar System, reduced within a circle two yards in diameter. Then, on every side, and above and below, an encompassing void of four miles, each inch in those miles standing again for ninety-three million miles. And then, in one direction, a single star.

Only one quite so near. Another in the Sun's "vicinity," known as 61 Cygni, would lie seven miles off, and the brilliant Sirius, not so brilliant on this tiny scale, would be farther still. Only about twenty stars are known to be nearer than one million times the distance of our Sun — which here would mean nearer than one million inches, or nearly sixteen miles.

Others would have to be placed at distances of twenty miles, thirty miles, fifty miles, one hundred miles, one or two or more thousand miles. It is not easy to conjecture where one would have to stop.

That the Starry System — our great Universe — has limits some-where can hardly be doubted. But to define those limits with any kind of precision is not possible. It is believed that some dim stars, barely visible, may lie ten thousand times as far away as our Sun's next neighbor, Alpha Centauri, and this would give a line from the center of our reduced Universe of thirty-five thousand miles.

Suppose that the limits did lie there. Thirty-five thousand miles, each way outward, would mean a diameter for the whole of seventy thousand miles. Imagine a starry system seventy thousand miles across from side to side, each separate inch in all those tens of thousands of miles representing ninety-three million miles of true distance!

And somewhere in the midst, our small Solar System, just two yards across, separated from all other stars in every direction by a wide blank of four miles.

This would be stupendous enough. But we have no reason for thinking that the limits do lie there. The System may extend twice as far, four times as far.

As for the numbers of suns, great and small, which, taken all together, make up this wonderful Universe, who can estimate them? Yet estimates have been made, and one thing is certain — that the grand reality does not fall short of human ideas.

Seen by us, without any help from magnifying glasses, only a few thousands of stars are visible. But with even a small telescope, the numbers spring to hundreds of thousands. With more powerful lenses, leap follows leap, from hundreds of thousands to millions, and to tens of millions.

Nor does the widening of our heavenly landscape stop there. When the greatest telescope yet made has done its utmost, we have not reached the limit. Beyond the range of telescopic vision, stars beyond stars still lie in countless hordes, invisible to human eyes, yet within reach of human powers. For then steps in photography; and suns innumerable — suns never yet seen, and perhaps never to be seen from this world by the eyes of men — stamp their feeble image on the photographic plate.

Then higher still the numbers mount, till one hundred millions of stars, two hundred millions of stars, are reckoned to belong to our Universe. And who may say how many more?

IV. – IMMENSITY – AND MAN

The bewildering immensity of our Universe, the utter insignificance of our Earth — these have been a difficulty with many minds.

It has been asked, not scornfully, but with real anxiety: "How can we suppose that the Creator of all things, the Maker of such a Universe as this — even if there are no other universes — can pay attention to our tiny world, a mere speck in Creation? How can we dream that the Eternal will stoop to care for us individually, will hear and answer our prayers, when He has tens of millions of glorious suns to claim His thoughts?"

A very old question, powerfully expressed two thousand years ago or more by a patriarch in trouble. Little though he dreamt what the Universe really means, he did see something of the problem. And so he asked —

"What is man that Thou shouldest magnify him? and that Thou shouldest set Thine Heart upon him? and that Thou shouldest visit him every morning, and try him every moment?"[18]

He does not seem to have questioned the fact that God did magnify man, did set His Heart upon him, did visit him every morning, did keep trying and testing him all through life. His wondering query was, rather, how could this be? What was there in man which should make his Maker so lovingly regard and care for him? Some now, echoing the patriarch's words, ask also in addition, "But is it truly so?"

18   Job vii.

Beyond question, our Earth is very, very small, and the Universe is very, very large.

Not long since, a certain idea came up and was much talked about as likely to help in this difficulty. It was suggested as possible — some said, extremely probable — that our Earth lay just exactly at the center of the great System of Stars.

People liked the notion. It seemed to invest our tiny globe with a certain fortuitous importance; the importance, not of size or of radiance, but of position. If only we might think of our Earth as occupying that place, and of all the rest of the Universe as perhaps circling round her!

But this we cannot do. There is not the smallest reason for imagining that the stars of the Universe circle round us. It *may* be that they circle round some great center, though whether they do, or if they do, what and where that center is, no man can say. In any case, our tiny Earth — nay, more, our comparatively unimportant Sun — would be powerless. No controlling and overmastering power belongs to either, to fit them for such a post. And that is what is really meant by the importance of a "central position."

Surely, we are ascribing here to God very small human ideas of importance and worth. What are size and weight and position to Him Who made all things? — to Him Who holds the Universe in the hollow of His Hand?

Do we not see how constantly in the past He did not often call on the great and powerful nation, or the prominent and important individual, to do His work? Did He not commonly choose the smaller nation, the younger and less-esteemed brother, the humble and neglected person, for His purposes? The fallacy of the above notion seems to lie in a half-expressed idea that the Divine Creator and Father of all values a world for its diameter, or reckons the worth of a sun by its weight.

Once more I should like to quote Dr. Pritchard. We were together outside his observatory at Oxford, where he had been explaining many matters of interest; and I must have said something relating to the question of our Earth's unimportance. He replied with emphasis —

"You think a great deal too much of mere bigness! I find as much in one little flower in my garden to arouse my wonder and awe as in all the stars of the Universe!"

And was he not right? Do we not all think far too much of mere bigness?

Can we imagine that with God size is anything, or distance is anything? He is everywhere and in everything. And if with Him one thousand years are as one day, may we not also believe that with Him a billion miles may be but as one mile, and that the mightiest blazing sun may rank in importance as at least no higher than our Earth?

Since He saw fit — so it seems to us! — to choose this little world as the battlefield of contending forces of good and evil, what are we to question His will?

The make of a little leaf, of a small flower-petal, is as marvellous, as full of mystery, as the construction of a starry system. In trying to reckon up the number of suns, or in trying to get to the ultimate specks of matter in one feather of a butterfly's wing, we are alike brought up by baffling walls, through which we cannot pass.

Does it matter at all whether the Earth is large or small? Or whether its position is at the center of the Universe, as some have maintained, or away in the outskirts, as some now incline to believe? Wherever we are, we may be sure that "we cannot drift beyond His love and care."[19]

"Life is a very little thing, but it is the only thing that counts."[20] These words seem just to give the right clue. Surely, a little child of Earth counts for more in the Divine Sight than the hugest masses of lifeless matter whirling through space!

True, they are wonderful, these vast suns and countless worlds. True also, many more of the latter than we imagine may have their inhabitants. But that does not touch the fact that "GOD SO LOVED — " this particular world. You know how the sentence goes on. Could any distinction of size or position rank beside that distinction?

As for what all the millions of suns may be for and what may be the precise object of their existence, here again we are at fault. We do

19   Whittier.
20   T. R. Glover.

know that they were not made, as our forefathers once fondly thought, wholly and solely to give light to us in the absence of our Moon. Many may already be centers of light and life to surrounding worlds. Many are perhaps undergoing preparation for such work, or for other work, in the far future. We cannot so much as guess what unknown purposes they may be destined to fulfill in ages yet to come.

One thing at least is clear to us now, and that in itself is not unsatisfying: "The heavens declare the glory of God, and the firmament showeth His handiwork."